O_2

Book one in the *Dylan Malloy* Series

Nic D'Alessandro

O_2

Book one in the *Dylan Malloy* Series

First published 2023

Published by Nic D'Alessandro

Website: https://nicdalessandro.com

ISBN paperback edition: 978-0-6451114-3-9

ISBN ebook edition: 978-0-6451114-2-2

A catalogue record for this book is available from the National Library of Australia

For Charlotte, Jack, Meg, Sarah, Steve and the many others who choose to rise above their circumstances each day.

No one saves us but ourselves.
No one can, and no one may.
We ourselves must walk the path.
– Buddha

1

Present day

O_2: 2% LOW

The angry readout beside my knee is blinking hard, begging for my attention. I stare at those tiny red numbers. That piss-weak reading of two percent is gonna flip to zero any second now. But my lungs are already there. *They burn.* My body screams for more air—for oxygen.

This isn't the time to be looking down, though. Not now.

I jerk my head upwards. I gotta look … I just have to—

Blink.

Disbelief at the massive sea of lights out there in the dark: white, green, blue, and red. Some are flashing as if sharing the panic with me. A few strobing. Most seem fixed in space and the faraway ones shimmer and shake.

"Now, Dylan. Do it now," Anderson says, his voice even more raspy and strained.

My left thumb is near this tiny black button. Not right on it, but near enough. One press and it will be done. No going back.

More lights are flicking past. Faster. Bright and piercing. A row of pinpoint green ones ahead. There's a dark space behind with lines of tiny white lights out to the horizon, like a freakish oblong-shaped black hole pulling me forward.

"Two hundred," the other voice says again. But, unlike Anderson, this guy still sounds calm. He seems kinda stoned, too, like I remember from years back.

I wheeze in a forced breath until my lungs scream back at me, then chance another quick look down at the bottle:

O_2: 1% LOW

Whatever.

One press of this button near my thumb and it won't matter. Nothing will.

How crazy is this? I spent years dreaming of sitting in this seat, and now I'm finally here. Irony is, this is probably the last thing I'll ever do. I'll most likely be dead within the next minute. My chances of pulling off this crazy manoeuvre? About one-in-four, I reckon.

And even if I do survive, it probably won't matter. I could be dead in twenty-four hours, anyway. My chances of surviving the operation I'm supposed to have tonight are one-in-five.

And if by some miracle I make it through, I'm guessing I'll go six-feet-under within a year. Around half the people like me do.

"Dylan, *now*!" Anderson's lost all his cool. His panic is real, which is nuts, 'coz he's not even here.

The line of green lights is closer now. Really close.

Should I be asking: *why me?* I could ask that question if I had the time. That bitch—that very question—has been following me like a stray dog. Any other dumb prick who found themselves where I am right now, if they were doing what I'm about to do, they'd be asking, *why … the … hell … me …* if they weren't too busy screaming.

Faces float in and out of my head. People who give a damn. People who matter to me. Never thought I'd get all the stuff about others, but maybe … maybe she was right. Just wish I could've told her before—

The green lights flick under the nose.

This is insane. Death is right here, but I feel … alive.

Nothing for it, then.

I press the black button.

2

Five years earlier

Boots. Tan coloured. Scuffed toes, all dusty. One of them is poking me in the chest.

The soil blazes orange-red and is super close.

I squint hard to get these tortured eyes to focus.

Frayed elastic sides on the boots. There's two legs above—thin denim poles going skyward. A torn knee. A humongous belt buckle shines overhead.

Things are coming back. My head's throbbing like it'll burst. Throat is sandpaper. Sunburn bites.

A chequered shirt is above that buckle. Red, white, and pale green.

Then a skinny black neck.

Then stubble, lots of it. Silver and wiry.

The sun torches my eyes from above the stranger's head. So strong I can't make out his eyes.

"Thought you was dead, young fella." He crouches low. His half-smile shows crooked teeth in a wrinkled black face. Breath stinks of god knows what.

I try to stand up, but my strength has gone and sitting like a crashed insect on this orange dirt is all I can manage. Everything hurts and my lungs are on fire. I plonk a hand on the soil to keep myself from falling.

There's a deep, pulsing mechanical rumble in the near distance, and an eighteen-wheeler materialises as my eyes lose their blur. The machine's got two trailers—a road train. Beyond the truck, there's endless orange dirt shimmering away in the heat.

What was I thinking?

He slouches further on his haunches and cocks his head. "What you thinking, mate, out here on this bloody back road with just a backpack?"

I go to answer him, but my throat and tongue are not playing ball. My damned cough—the blasted asthma thing that won't go away—is building again in my lungs. I'll be spluttering and wheezing like a steam engine any second, guaranteed.

"When did ya drink last?"

I shrug my shoulders and stare.

Hints of a nightmare are pulling at my head. There's some crazy memory I don't want to think about, but it's bubbling below the surface like it only just happened. Flashes of vision: another vehicle and an old guy driving it. But not the guy who's talking to me now. A different bloke. More blips of memory … I'm alone on some lonely, gravel road a long way from anywhere or anyone. Alone in a stranger's campervan. Just a dream? Coulda been. But the fear knifing my guts me tells me this nightmare might have been real.

"C'mon. Let's get you up," says the man. He goes to put his hands under my armpits. His touch is like an electric shock.

But why?

O2

Nausea now. A sharp wave of sick pushing up from below and it wants the light of day. I fight the urge and push it down.

More flickers of memory as I stagger to my feet. The sickening smile of the other old guy, the one in the campervan. Yeah, the other guy earlier today. It's coming back, but I push those memories down—just like the vomit.

Being alone is less risky, that's coming clear, but I can't stay out here on my own like this. I probably would've died if this truckie hadn't found me.

I can see beyond the truck now as my eyes come good. There's nothing out there. Nothing anywhere in any direction. Reminds me of photos I've seen of Mars.

This truckie is my only option.

• • • • • • • • • • •

Getting into this monster truck isn't easy. My legs aren't cooperating, so he tries to push me up and into the cab. He's stronger than he looks.

"I'm fine," I croak, pulling away from his upstretched hands. Reckon I've had a complete gutful of intense old blokes for one week, but at least I know how to pick a creep when I see one now.

This old truckie, though, he doesn't seem to fit that profile. He just goes hands-on-hips, shrugs, and says, "Righto." He seems okay so far, and his face is like, trustworthy?

Hope so.

I grab the far edge of the passenger seat and somehow drag myself into the cab.

We start rolling down the dead-straight highway. I wonder how far to the next town. I try to peer ahead, but there's nothing but bitumen, white lines, dirt, and scrub. May as well settle in for the long haul.

Time doesn't seem to exist out here. I've got no idea if we've been driving for minutes or hours when I feel myself nodding off—or is it waking up?

Aunt Cheryl's face sticks with me in my daydreams. Can't shake it. That final look the last time I saw her.

Did she make it? Is she okay?

I push her picture outa my head and fight the urge to sleep.

Stay awake. Must stay … awake …

••••••••••••

Grab the armrest. Hard. Heave in a sharp breath.

Awake again.

Fighting sleep just doesn't work.

We're still rolling down the highway. But I'm okay. I'm safe.

The frickin urge to cough is still with me. I've learned to wheeze in a sharp breath, silently, and then grip and hold the instinct to bark, then expel the air slowly through my lips. My chest jumps a fraction, but not enough for anyone to notice.

"Ya must be dry as a dead dingo's donger." I glance over to see he's got one hand on the steering wheel and the other extended toward me with an aluminium can pinched between a finger and a thumb. "Get that into yer cake hole."

Embarrassed, my words come out croaky-as. "Thanks, but the water was enough."

"Bullshit. Get drinkin'. That's Nullarbor medicine."

I accept the can; it's ice cold on my fingers. The label says GO WEST XXX BITTER. "It's not medicine, it's … it's beer."

"Same thing. Keep drinking."

Okay, then. Do as the doctor says.

Bitter? Sure-as-hell is. Only tasted beer a few times before, and just the light stuff. This is more like cough medicine, but it'll do.

White lines flick beneath us. Many minutes, too. Could've been hours.

"Where you from?" he asks.

"Melbourne."

"Hmm. Big city fella. Where you goin'?"

"Perth."

"One big city to the next, ay? Some walkabout you on for a white boy."

Walkabout? If only he knew.

Another scull of beer. He's right. Bush medicine, this.

The old truckie keeps his eyes on the road. He seems right at home on his big, bouncy seat and effortlessly in control of this enormous rig. One hand is tweaking the steering wheel with a couple of fingertips and his other hand rests easily beside him when it's not flicking a gear lever. He shimmies in his seat to scratch his back with no hands, and says, "So, you was gonna walk the Nullarbor alone with a backpack and no water?"

"That wasn't the plan."

His whole upper-body shakes as he laughs. Each *hah* sound he makes rolls out his mouth in slow motion with a deep, gravelly sound and a weird gap between. And when they all come to a stop, eventually, he says, "Oh, you had a *plan,* did ya?"

"Yep."

"How old are ya? Eighteen?"

"Nineteen."

"Any kid walking Melbourne to Perth has no plan. Yer dreamin', mate."

His face comes back to me again, the old arsehole in the campervan. His sick smile as he'd offered me a lift…

I shake my head. "I wasn't walking it. Not until yesterday."

"Sounds like a story," he grunts. "Righto, come on then, spill ya guts."

No one needs to hear my story. I'm out here 'coz I've moved on and I'm leaving the crap back where it belongs, thanks all the same. And anyway, I *do* have a plan. Lots of things haven't gone my way, and there're people who think I'm just some geek loser with no future, but I'm going to show them. They're going to eat their words. I'm gonna make something of myself. I'm going to be someone, and Perth is where it all might happen. So yeah, I have a plan. I just don't have all the … details, yet.

So, I shake my head, look out at the flat horizon, and say, "Nah. It's a long story. Too long."

"Look at that road, mate." He points a gnarled finger out beyond the windscreen. "We won't see Perth for twenty hours. I got the time if you got the story."

The distances on the Nullarbor are insane. Longest I've ever been in a vehicle is six hours Melbourne to Canberra with mum, but six hours out here would be like a drive to the shops.

"Are you going to keep driving, like … non-stop?" I ask, hoping this might divert the guy from his need to hear my story.

"Except for fuel, food-n-piss stops, yeah," he says with a dry grin. Then he waggles a crooked finger at the windscreen like he's telling someone off. "Just don't tell my logbook, ay. I go slower than the other truckies, but I make good time by the end."

And right then, another truck—an eighteen-wheeler with a single trailer—comes thundering past us. It overtakes with a blast of its horn, and the rig's slipstream whacks us hard for a second.

"I give 'em the shits, the other drivers," he says, his remaining teeth glowing again. "Me name's Coolanyarra, but they call me Pothole."

I'm guessing his nickname isn't meant to be cute.

"Yep, *Pothole*," he continues. "I'm something to avoid on the highway. An old black fella driving too slow."

I ask him how long he's been a truckie and how he got into it, and all that. For the next while he tells me the headlines of his life story and some of the detail too. There's a bit more to this guy than I first thought, which is good because then we don't have to talk about me. Except, he stops mid-sentence.

"So, you got a name?"

Keep it short-'n'-sweet.

"Dylan."

"Pleased to meet ya, Dylan, the man with no plan." He chuckles again. "Anyway, on with your story."

Damn, he hasn't forgotten. Jeez, is this show-and-tell in primary school or something? Talking about myself isn't what I'm into, never has been. But Pothole's super-open and told me more about himself than I expected.

"Okay. Um, yesterday I was—"

"Nah, mate. Not *yesterday*," he interrupts. "Start from the start."

The start?

I take another swig of beer. Dutch courage. Nullarbor medicine. My head flicks through my sorry life, desperately searching for something to say. But what? Yesterday's road trip, the dramas of this week, these past few crappy years?

My mind just goes straight to the events of three years ago … the thing I don't talk about. I pull it back. We're not going there. No frickin way. I just need to give this guy something to keep him off my case, like, something not too deep or meaningful.

Pothole's fingers are tapping the steering wheel in a slow rhythm. He's not going anywhere, and he's obviously got all the time in the world.

I clear my throat as a usable memory finally clicks in. "Okay. So, a few years back…"

3

A further four years earlier

"Velocity-one-heavy. Descend three thousand, turn left two-two-five to intercept the two-five-left localiser."

I read back the air traffic controller's instruction, "Descend three thousand, left two-two-five, Velocity-one-heavy."

The approach controller rattles off more instructions, but I ignore them. In this congested airspace, the controller is firing radio calls to many aircraft as they approach Los Angeles International, known for short as LAX. But I listen only for our unique callsign: *Velocity-one-heavy*.

Time for a deep breath as I dial the altitude setting down to three thousand feet, swing the heading bug left to two-twenty-five degrees, and watch the 777's automation systems respond to my every command. A quick glance again at the instrument approach chart for Runway 25-Left to double-check distances and altitudes on the approach profile—all good.

"Dylan." A voice somewhere in the distance.

The localiser indicator on my primary flight display is alive now. It's moving steadily towards the centre. The big jet rolls left in response to the instrument landing system signal that guides us down to the runway.

As I wait for another break in the radio traffic, I can't help grinning. These American controllers are among the best. They handle ridiculous amounts of traffic, all easy and calm with their cool Californian accents.

The break comes, and I hit the transmit switch. "Established two-five left, Velocity-one-heavy."

And as I finish my last word, the controller is right there with me. "Velocity-one-heavy, speed one-seventy to LIMMA, contact tower one-two-zero-niner-five, g'night."

We're heading down now as I read back his instruction. The 777's autothrottle is moving the thrust levers back to reduce our airspeed towards a hundred and seventy knots. Flaps *25*. Gear *down*. The localiser and glideslope indicators are dead centre on my display—we're smack on the approach. The runway approach lights appear through scattered clouds ahead.

"Dylan."

Ignore that. *Dylan* is not my callsign, not right now.

I have the *120.95* frequency pre-set in the primary radio unit, so I hit the transfer switch. The tower frequency isn't as busy, and I press the transmit button again. "LAX Tower, g'day, Velocity-one-heavy, I L S two-five-left."

"*Dylan*!" Still distant, but louder this time.

"Velocity-one-heavy, evenin', wind two-six-zero at eight, runway two-five-left, clear to land."

"Two-five-left, clear to land, Velocity-one-heavy," I read back. Fast but cool.

This is it. In thirty seconds, I'll press the *Autopilot-disconnect* button on the flight yoke, then I'll hand-fly the rest of the approach and landing. After a fourteen-hour flight from Sydney with the autopilot flying the plane most of that time, this is my chance to show this 777 who's in charge. Who's pilot-in-command. These final few miles to the runway are the cream on the aviation cake and everything I've ever trained for.

But there's a warmth behind me and a creepy stench of beer. Someone's hand has grabbed me on the shoulder and it's shaking me hard.

I stick up my right hand in protest. "Not now."

"Yes, *now*!" the voice from behind booms.

I hit the *Autopilot-disconnect* button and hear the *whoop-whoop* confirmation as the autopilot cuts out. I grab the control yoke. This is where I do that pilot stuff. This is when I prove *I* am the man.

"Dylan, show me some bloody respect!"

A hard finger-poke stabs into my right shoulder. I have to turn and face him.

Tony is my aunt's partner and a total meathead. Medium height, just, and built solid; he looks like he could take some decent whacks and not even flinch. You'd think he'd have a good 'ol beer gut at forty-eight with how he sinks beers, but he's somehow avoided that one. It's his face that really gets your attention though: chiselled like a statue, sunken cheeks and eyes, caterpillar eyebrows, and a freaky hard stare.

"What!" I say, trying not to flinch under his glare.

"I asked you to put out the garbage bins." He shakes an index finger at me. "One job you had. You've done stuff-all since you got here and can't even do that!"

"I will, I will. I need to finish this. Give me five minutes—"

"Five minutes, my arse."

I look back at the main screen. The runway threshold is close now, but I can still land this thing despite the frickin interruption. Tony can just wait.

"The garbage truck's comin' down the street. *Stop* what you're doing and get those bins out," he yells.

"I can't, I—"

"You're what? Stuck on this bloody computer again."

There seems to be no way of shutting this guy up, so I hit the pause button, hard. "I gotta finish this flight. Five more minutes!"

Tony leans in past my shoulder and takes a confused glance at the screen. The two caterpillars above his eyes are angled-in hard now, joined in the middle, and bristling. "Flight? What the … you playing pilots or something?"

"It's not a game." I fold my arms as tight as they'll go. "It's flight simulation."

He's probably got no idea what those words even mean.

He stands back and roars out a single laugh. "Hah! I don't give a flying fark about your *simulation*, whatever it is. The bins, *now*!"

I break his stare and grab the mouse. "Okay. Alright. *Jeez*."

I'm mega pissed-off, but there's no use going on. I hover the mouse pointer over the *Disconnect* button for a millisecond, and click it. The *dah-doh* chime confirms my simulator session is done. Fifteen hours all down the virtual drain.

••••••••••

Missed it by ten seconds. The garbage truck is pulling away as I tear down the driveway, pulling the two bins behind me.

"Hey, wait!" I yell, pointlessly waving my arm at the departing truck. It just keeps on lumbering around the corner. Damn, Tony will be even more triggered now. He's a cockhead at the best of times, but this'll hype him right up.

Oh well, screw him. I tried. I do a 180-turn and head back towards the house. Serves him right for ruining everything. I spent hours on that flight—planning, setting it up, flying it. Sure, I wasn't there every minute, and I took breaks while the simulated 777 cruised over the Pacific Ocean—autopilots are good for that—but it was just me echoing real life. On a flight, the captain has first and second officers to manage the plane during the boring bits and he can sleep, eat, whatever. I did the same. But arriving into LAX and nailing the approach and landing was meant to be my reward. I've been flying my PC-flight simulator online for years; spent hundreds of hours learning all there is to know. The 737 and 777 airliners are like old mates to me now. Not that dumb Tony, who could barely hold down a job at a servo, would know anything about those things.

I fly online in the VATSIM network whenever I can. It's thousands of virtual pilots and air traffic controllers from all over the world who run a virtual-reality aviation environment—all free and volunteer-run. As real as it gets, without being real.

One day I'll be doing the *real* thing—an airline pilot—as my day job. There'll be no interruptions from cockhead Tony then.

Speaking of which, I look up as I near the corner of the house where the bins are stored and there he is. Waiting for me.

I try to soften the blow. "Sorry, Tony. I ah … I just missed it."

He scowls and scratches his balls. *Gross.* "That'd explain why you're still drag'n them bins then, ay?"

I focus on the ground. "Yeah."

Cockhead.

"Is this how you go at home, at your mum's place?"

I shrug. If I don't say too much, he'll run out of steam.

"S'pose that comes with being an only child, don't it?"

I don't reply, just go to move past him. He sticks one foot out, blocking my path.

"Talkin' to you, ya fuckin' spoiled brat. Don't lift a finger around here. Just cruising along eat'n all our food."

All the food Aunt Cheryl buys, you mean.

"Sorry." I talk to the ground. I've become good at playing meek with Tony. It's the best way to keep him off my back. He grunts and removes his foot, and I line the bins up neatly next to the paint peeling fibro. "Next week I—"

"Next week you'll be out on your ear if *I* got anything to do with it." He jabs a dirty finger at me. "And next time your mum pisses off outta the country to go save the world, or whatever she does, she can drop your ungrateful arse off somewhere else. *You're not wanted here,* got it?"

His hands are shaking a bit now. Fingers trembling as they flex. There's a dribble of spit at the corner of his mouth and if his eyes squint any harder, they'll shut completely.

I got no idea what to say to him. This is the second time I've stayed with Tony and Aunt Cheryl, and the first time he pretty much ignored me the whole three weeks. I haven't seen him as pissed as this before.

I really wish Cheryl would get home about now. I glance at the street, but all is quiet. Just a row of identical, yellowing grass yards with boxy houses and the odd car wreck as decoration. No people. Not even a neighbouring dog around to witness whatever the hell is about to happen.

What do I do? Walk away? Do I leave?

He steps towards me and I automatically jerk backwards, drag in a ragged breath, and raise my hands in front of my chest. I can feel the raspy heat of a cough building way down low and I make a strangled, choking sound.

He chuckles and pushes off from the house, advancing. "Not such a smart arse now, are ya?" The finger is back up and this time he's shoving it hard in my chest. I take a step back. There's a mean glint to his eye I've not seen before.

"I'm gonna teach you some proper respect, you little piece 'a—"

The sound of my phone stops him mid-sentence. The loud, ditsy ringtone version of 'Danger Zone' seems perfect for this moment.

"It's uh … mum," I stammer, wrenching the phone out of my pocket. And excellent timing she has too. She'd called three times earlier this afternoon, but I couldn't talk to her then. Not on the school bus. No privacy there, plus the senior guys would've stirred the crap out of me. But I've been saved by the ringtone this time, so I press the *Talk* icon.

"Hey," I say, chirpy as I can.

"Dylan. *Finally*! How are you, honey?" she says.

"Good."

Tony is looking pissed, but he won't do anything while Mum is on the phone. I have no idea how I know this, but I've seen the way he is when she's around and he barely says boo.

"Just good?"

I can hear the sounds of public announcements in the background. Maybe she's at the airport. God, I hope it's time for her to come home.

"Yep." I glance at Tony, but he's slinked back. Shoved his hands in his pockets, all bravado shrivelled up like a popped balloon. He shakes his head and stomps off. I want to hurl the phone at his head. *Scumsucker.*

Mum is saying something, but I don't catch it. "Sorry … uh, the line's not good."

"I said, do you miss me?" She's raised her voice, on the verge of yelling.

I can feel the cough coming for another strike and rub my chest with my left fist. "You at the airport to come home?"

Please.

She laughs. "I'll take that as a yes. And no, I'm not, but I am in the hotel lobby waiting for my lift to the airport. We're heading for Amsterdam. I'll be home on Friday."

The excitement in her voice is clear. Mum likes her job and the travel, but gets homesick after a few weeks away. Then I'll get lots of texts and calls from her, like this one. Her career and me are all she's got, I think.

"Good," I mumble.

I fully miss mum, to be honest. She has this job with the government and works overseas sometimes. She's been in the Netherlands for four weeks working at this Hague place, or something. So, yeah, it's been a while, and while I don't mind staying with Aunt Cheryl, I've just about had enough of this Tony dickhead. Today, I hate to admit it, but he was scaring me.

"You okay?" There's concern in her voice.

Great, now I'm being a big baby.

"Yeah, I'm cool." I wander down the driveway, as though moving will inject some energy into my voice. "I was just going to go stay at my mate's place for a couple of days, do some gaming. But I guess if you're coming home, I can't."

"Ah, c'mon! Don't get *too* excited to see your dear mum."

I can picture her when she's saying those words. One of her hands would have been up and pleading. Her head would tilt to the right and her eyes would've rolled a bit. My mum's got these eyes—soft and wide. But they can see through anything and anyone, even from the other side of the world.

"How's things at Cheryl's place?"

My answer doesn't happen. I go to say something, but my throat jams up and I cough and splutter.

"Tell me you've got your puffer with you, Dylan."

"Of course," I wheeze.

"Use it now, please. Your asthma sounds like it's flaring again."

More like Tony's flaring. Bit hard to breathe right when someone is threatening to beat the crap out of you.

"Mum—"

"*Now*, Dylan. You've got to take care of yourself, and if it gets worse, get Cheryl to take you to a doctor. Don't risk another run-in with bronchitis."

She's right, the bronchitis sucks, so I put my phone down on the driveway fence and do the deed.

"*There*. Happy now?" I whinge into the phone.

She ignores me, but doesn't ignore my detour. "Aunt Cheryl's, how's things?"

I glance up at the house. The front door is shut and no sign of Tony. Maybe I could sneak back into my room and he'll leave me be. Surely, Cheryl will be back soon.

"Dylan?" Mum says.

"Yeah. Fine."

She sighs. "You don't sound like yourself."

"It's fine, really." I scuff my shoes against the driveway and think about bolting to my room, but that means walking past the lounge room, and possibly Tony.

"Is Tony still giving you grief?"

"Sometimes. Look, Mum, I gotta go. I—"

"That's a *yes*, then." Her voice rises a notch. She's getting pissed. And that's not good, because if this trend continues, her Irish heritage will really come through. The verbal turbulence will be short, but also full-on hectic.

"Really, it's okay," I say, calm as I can. "You'll be home Friday."

"Yes, and we can talk more when I get there. Next time we might find you somewhere else to stay when I travel. But two more days, then you and I can head home to Canberra."

Two days sounds like a lifetime to me, but I'll just have to stick it out, I guess.

"Dylan? Still there?"

"Yeah. What flight are you on?" I ask.

"Hold on ... ah, our flight number is ... K X seventy-two."

"Right. I'll keep an eye on your progress."

"With your flight-tracker thingy?" she says, giggling. "You really *are* an aeroplane geek."

"That's me."

And she's right. I am an aviation geek, through-and-through. It comes with its benefits though, like, I know the airline she's on, and their history, and I can check she's okay all the way home.

And it's funny, but even thinking about flying and aeroplanes lifts my spirits.

"Well, I gotta go, honey," she says. "Our ride's turned up. I'll be thinking of you all the whole way home."

"Cool."

"Love you."

"You too, Mum."

I disconnect the call and suddenly realise when Tony made me pull out of that flight, the LAX tower controller would have thought

I was a complete loser. The people watching me on my *Twitch* streaming channel probably do now too.

Cockhead.

4

Present day, Nullarbor Plain

"So, that's why you was at your aunt's place?" Pothole asks.

"Yeah. I had to stay with her. She's the only other family I had."

I didn't mean to tell him all that. Not about family and stuff.

"Had?" he sort of asks, but sort of doesn't. "What about a dad, you got one-a-them?"

A part of me is saying *shut up, Dylan, keep your stuff to yourself.* Another part's saying *who cares, you nearly died today, and you'll never see this guy again, anyway.*

So, I swallow hard and cross my arms. "Mum only told me my dad was some surfer-dude … from the United States. They had a one-night hook-up in Bali and two months later, she found out she was pregnant with me. Mum only knew the guy's first name, and she never saw him again."

"Sounds like your mum's had a tough run, ay?"

A tough run? Jeez.

I melt further into my seat and let my head lean on the side window and bounce along with the bumps. The guide posts on this side of the road rush at the truck, one-by-one, then disappear quicker than they came. A squished kangaroo flashes past, its sun-baked blood and guts spread half on the bitumen and half on the orange dirt.

To be real, I'd rather just think about that sucker of a kangaroo and nothing else right now. Not my mum, or dad, or Cheryl, or Melbourne, or whatever my life was back there. It's not like I don't think about my mum. I can't stop the memories in my head and flashes of her face sometimes, so I've given up trying. And I wonder about my dad, too, every-now-and-then. Who is he? Where is he? Is the guy even alive?

But Pothole doesn't need to know any of that crap right now, so I just fob him off. "Guess so," I mumble at the window. "Long story, like I said."

He points out at the road again with another knowing look, but this time Pothole seems to pick up I'm in a bind and changes the subject. "If you like planes so much, then why not fly to Perth?"

"That was back then," I say, and instantly realise my words sound lifeless and hard.

Back then…

"What was?" he asks.

Does he ever give up?

"Planes. Aviation. Being a pilot. All that." I keep my eyes locked outside the truck on the endless desert.

"And now?"

"It's not for now." I try to sound all noble and final about it. "Not for me. I'm done with it."

"Hmm." He scratches his stubble and gives his bottom jaw a stretch. "Sounds heavy."

I'm thankful for the ride, but I'm stuck here with nowhere to go and this Pothole guy seems to have a sixth sense, or something. But he has no idea, really. No idea how talking about those stupid old dreams—flying planes, becoming an airline pilot—still kicks me in the guts, even now. It's all gone and needs to stay *gone*. Talking about it just hardens the gut-kick.

I go for another sip of beer, but the can's empty no matter how far I tilt it back.

"Chuck that in the back. There's more tinnies in the cooler," he says, pointing into the sleeper with a thumb. "Help yourself."

"Thanks."

"You feelin' any better?"

"Think so," I say, relieved he seems to have dropped the interrogation.

"Good to hear. We'll stop and get some tucker soon."

I nod. I am hungry now that I've thought about it.

But the cogs of Pothole's brain keep turning like the wheels of his truck, only slower. "So, this Uncle Tony fella—"

I flick my head from the road to him and glare. "He's not my uncle. I am *not* related to that arsehole, no way."

"Right. Anyway. This Tony fella. Sounds like a right sump-plug."

"Yep."

"Ah well. You must have been laughin' when your mum got home?"

I go to answer him, but nothing's there. No words. No thoughts. Nothing. I look out my window and tighten my hold on the armrest.

Get a grip, Dylan. … keep it together … do … not … crack.

Pothole isn't interested in my silence, but thankfully he returns to his first subject. "So what's he about then, this Tony?"

"He um ..." I wipe my eyes with a quick swipe of a sleeve as I think about what to say, and hope Pothole doesn't notice.

....

Four years earlier, Melbourne

The commotion is plain to hear even before I turn off the footpath into the driveway. Tony's voice is booming. Aunt Cheryl's isn't as loud, but it shrieks and cuts right through. The whole thing's like a contest between a psycho rottweiler and an angry cockatoo.

Tony works at a car parts factory and he does a lot of night shifts. Which is good, 'coz it means I'm awake when he's asleep, and vice-versa. But his shifts have been cut-back and I'm guessing that means money's tight.

"I'll farkin do whatever the hell I want," he yells, his words slow and slurred.

"Tell me what I don't know," Aunt Cheryl screeches back, "you useless piece of *shit!*"

Tony's always been a drinker and he can hold it pretty well. Lately, though, he's drinking a lot more. He comes home pissed a few nights-a-week. It's good when he's full-on pissed 'coz he'll drop on the couch and sleep and snore till the next day. But if he's half-pissed, watch out. He'll be looking for an argument or a full-blown fight. He doesn't hit anyone, I don't think, but I stay well out of his way.

"Don't you talk that way to me, *bitch*! I make the money in this 'ere house and don't you bloody forget it."

"Yeah, you make it, then you piss it down the drain and it's *me* who has to deal with the debt collectors."

O2

There's a break in the yelling as I near the back door. Has Aunt Cheryl shut him up for now? But, no. There's the flick of a bottle lid, a hiss of rushing air, and a *clink* as the lid hits the tiled floor.

The angry cockatoo starts again, "Well that's bloody great, ay? Have another beer, Tony. Yeah, that'll fix everything."

I open the door, step inside, and an object shoots past me. A flash of something brown and shiny. Glass shatters on the other side of the kitchen.

Tony's standing to my left, breathing hard and fast. His hands are trembling.

Aunt Cheryl's on my right, all wide-eyed and her mouth is half-open. She's frozen to her spot. And then she sees me. "Dylan. Ah … hi. How was school?"

I look at Tony. Look at the broken glass. Then at her. "Fine, thanks."

She tries to smile, but it slips and slides off her face. Things here are anything but fine. The air feels heavy, everyone's on edge and wondering what will happen next. Should I say something to stop whatever's going on? Should I rescue Aunt Cheryl from this?

But before I can think of what to do, Tony storms past me and curses as he disappears out the back door.

I turn to Aunt Cheryl. "Are you ok?"

She's still got this pretend smile across her face. "Of course. It's all good. I dropped a bottle. Silly me!"

Now I'm faking a smile too, and I reckon I look as demented as her. It's time to sidestep out of here and head for my room.

I fall on the bed. My throat is burning and my breaths are kinda shallow, like my lungs are only half-working. Happens every now and then. And I get this gross build-up in my chest sometimes and have to heave it up, often after a shower. Frickin asthma.

So, I take another hit from my puffer, stare at the ceiling, and try to slow my breathing. My room here is small and quiet. I'll escape into my computer for the rest of this arvo and leave the happy couple to it. They'll think I'm doing homework.

If I had any good mates around here, I'd escape to their place instead. But I'm only in Melbourne for a school-term while mum's away. The school here is not my usual and I keep to myself. I can cope on my own, for two more days, anyway.

I open the flight-tracker app on my phone, click on *EHAM*—Amsterdam Airport Schiphol—and search for mum's flight number on the departures. *KX72* is way down the list and scheduled to take off in the middle of the night our time.

I ditch the phone and go back to my computer. A series binge will get me through the rest of today.

I'll check mum's progress in the morning.

••••••••••

Present day, Western Australia

It's becoming clear why Pothole enjoys his life on the road. It's awesome sitting way up here on a big, air-cushioned padded chair above all the ordinary traffic. This perspective of being above the world and seeing everyone else down below is pretty cool, and a bit like flying, really. The ride's really smooth too, with only the even hum of the truck engine and the whine of many wheels behind and beneath us.

The big windscreen is like a mega TV playing a road movie that never ends, and right now the scenery is showing off as the sun gets lower and the heat shimmer in the distance seems even wonkier. We haven't seen another vehicle for ages. The road and a few wildlife warning signs are the only things telling me we're still on planet Earth.

As the scene outside rolls on past, the vibrations of the rig move in and through me. And I wonder again about Aunt Cheryl. Did that prick follow her? Did she even make it?

The white lines ahead are still dead-straight and flick past as regular as a heartbeat.

Flick ... flick ... flick ...

....

The sharp hiss of air-brakes hits my ears and our forward motion comes to a sudden end.

"Wake up, princess," Pothole says.

It's almost dark. The sky's going black with a streak of blue out to the west. However, there's a strange brightness nearby, with lines of fluorescent lights above and vehicle lights all over the place.

"Guess I fell asleep," I say, Captain Obvious like.

"Guess you did. Your dreamtime went for two hours, mate."

"Jeez."

"Hop out. There's a food place over there," he says, as he points somewhere and nowhere. "Find us a table. I'll get the rig fuelled up. Shouldn't be too long."

I hop down out of the truck, blink hard to adjust my eyes, and wander through the lines of vehicles and pumps. I find the diner, eventually, and push open the door. No need for a bell—the hinges shriek like a bird of prey.

And yeah, I'm right at home in this truck stop.

Not.

At six-foot tall and built pretty thin, I'm kinda stringy to the eye. I've tried a few things to gain weight and add some muscle, but nothing seems to work. The people here are ... different: built like brick shithouses and covered in tatts. And that's just the women.

Pothole finds me at the table, eventually. "I'm ordering a big brekkie. Want one?"

"Ah, yeah. Thanks."

It's the opposite of breakfast time, but I reckon times-of-day don't count for much here. Any food right now, anything half-decent, will do the trick.

An ancient song is whining away on crackly speakers in the background and seems right at home in this dive. There's this underlying odour of disinfectant mixed with fried food. And every time someone opens the door, I get this fresh blast of heat and diesel.

A bloke is chomping down on this epic burger and staring out at the nothingness like it's something. A man and a woman—in their forties, I'd say—are at the table opposite us. They haven't said a word to each other in ten minutes. The guy sips his coffee on autopilot, his attention occupied by some YouTube on a screen held in his other hand. She's doing similar, just typing away at her screen with a single finger. Guess their phones must be that much more exciting than each other. Textually frustrated.

"Food's comin', and coffee," Pothole says as he slides into the opposite seat.

"Thanks for that. Sounds good." I slap a twenty dollar note down in front of him.

"She's right, fella, I'm buying."

Um ... embarrassing.

"Nah," I say, "I got some money. It's cool."

He grabs the note with a shrug of his shoulders and shoves into his shirt pocket. "Your funeral. Thought you was broke?"

No surprise Pothole thinks I'm a homeless dude with no funds. I must've looked the part when he found me on the road earlier today. But, strange as it is, access to cash is the only thing that hasn't gone to the dogs for me so far.

"Nah. I'm okay for now," I say with all the confidence I can bluster. "Just chipping away at the inheritance."

I clamp my eyes in a hard blink. *Dammit, why did I just say those words?*

"That right—got lucky, did ya?"

"It's just a trust fund, and ah … it depends on how you define *lucky;* I suppose."

Pothole squints his eyes like he's searching mine and twists his jaw to one side.

I break his stare and make a start on my 8:50 PM breakfast.

The bloke near us shoves his chair back and heads for the entrance. His missus looks up from her phone, huffs hard, and shuffles off behind him. And still not a word's said between. As I watch them make their separate ways to their car, I'm wondering: what is it with these couples, like, why do they even bother? Maybe that's why my Mum seemed okay with staying single. Makes sense.

Pothole scratches his scalp and relaxes back against the split orange vinyl of his booth seat. "Bit young to be havin' a trust fund, aren't ya?" he says. "Must mean yer story's even more interesting."

Interesting?

My hands clench into tight fists and without even thinking, I whack them down hard on the table surface either side of my empty placemat. "What do you *think* it frickin means? They're dead! Gone! I got no one!"

"*Whoa* there big fella." He jerks up a hand, palm-out, as if he's signalling an out of control rig to come to a stop out on the highway. "Sorry. Just steady your horses, ay."

My outburst has got my lungs heaving and my chest burning. And I know what comes next: coughing, hacking, and lots of it. I shove back my chair, spin on my heel away from the table, and bolt for the men's loo at the other side of the diner.

I've had a complete gutful of all this talking, anyway.

But even as I fling open the door and disappear into the hoped-for peace and quiet of the loo, there are other voices in my head that still won't stop. I stretch out my hands and lean against the wall over the washbasin. Voices, conversations, things spoken, words regretted, thoughts never said. They stream into my mind like unwanted podcasts I can't turn off.

If only I'd done more. If only I'd said something. If only I'd used what I knew to save her.

"Forgive me, mum," I whisper to no one. "Please, forgive me."

5

Don't know how long I stayed in the dodgy loo, but eventually the putrid wafts from the ancient urinals in there had got to me. Too many users, too little aim.

As I come out the door and scan across the diner, I spot a nearby exit door to my left. Pothole's seated near the far wall with his back to me, his head down and leaning heavily on one of his palms. The temptation to bolt through the door and just see what comes is strong, but so is the knowledge of what's waiting for me out there: *nothing*.

"I'm sorry about before," Pothole says, as I slide as quiet as I can into my seat. "You don't need to tell me about your money and your family and all."

"It's fine," I lie, and waving it all away with the swipe of a hand. "Don't worry about it."

He blows out a slow breath. "I can pretty much tell how things woulda turned out with that Tony bloke, anyway. And I won't ask about your mum, and whatever happened, and that. I'll keep me sticky old nose out of it."

"Yep," I bite my lip. "Thanks."

"Just seems like you've had your fair share of hard times for a young fella."

I shrug.

He cocks his head to one side and gestures with both hands. "It's like the philosophy bloke once said: '*Life is fulla shit, when ya think about it*'."

Jeez.

I really don't want to know, but I hear myself asking, "Oh, really? Which philosopher said that?"

He waves a hand above his head in a circle. "I dunno. Monty … someone."

Our food arrives. The fat bloke plonks our tray down at the head of the table and limps off without a word.

Pothole hands me a plate and pours steaming black coffee into this huge mug. "Good thing is, if you've had ya fair share, then things can only get better from here."

Huh? I don't get it.

"Who says?" I ask.

"Pothole says." He stabs one of his three poached eggs with a fork. The golden fluid spurts and runs across his plate until it hits a piece of thick toast. "It's just, you know, the law of averages and that."

"Oh. Right."

So, he's just saying something to make me feel better. Had my share? He doesn't know the half of it. And the law of averages? I can't see how it's worked for my mum, or for Aunt Cheryl. Far from it, actually.

Pothole rolls-up a piece of bacon and plops it in his mouth, so I do the same. I thought I'd slept-off my road trip tiredness in the truck, but as we get stuck into our meals, the need for sleep is pestering me hard again.

"How long will it take us to get to Perth?"

"Should be there by midday tomorrow."

"Right."

"You got someone you're meeting there?"

I shift in my seat and feel the note from Aunt Cheryl still in my back pocket. She gave me the name and number of a woman she knows in Perth.

"Nope," I say.

··········

The rig is ploughing along the highway in the dark. The blackness out there is everywhere, and it's like we're in a tunnel that never ends.

You put dents in my pickup,
And my dog you just kicked-up,
So I'm feeling real mad,
But hey … it's okay, honey … I got you real bad.

I'm dying here. Pothole has been playing this country-and-western rubbish for what seems like hours. If these lyrics had been set to country rock, then maybe I could deal with it. But this is banjo-picking country music at its worst. And the singer, if that's what he is, sounds like a geriatric cat dying in a drain.

"Shoot me now," I grumble to myself.

"What?" says Pothole.

"Nothing."

"It's the music of life, fella. It'll do you good."

"What? Getting so depressed I want to blow my frickin head off?"

He shakes with silent laughter. "It's like what the philosopher said—"

"Not that again. Life sucks, yeah, yeah, blah, blah."

"Thing is, listening to country tells me some poor bugger's got it *way* worse than me." He presses a button and puts the country singer out of his misery. "Happy now?"

"Happier, yeah."

Only the sound of the engine and tyres again, but he pipes-up after a few minutes. "You still haven't told me how you got from Melbourne to being half-dead on the Nullarbor Plain yesterday."

"Oh, yeah … that bit." My memories of yesterday's happenings are all coming back now, sucks as it does.

……….

One day earlier, South Australia

It'd taken until Wirrulla, this tiny town in the middle of outback nowhere, before I really thought about what was happening. The forty-degree heat, the four blocks of bare civilisation, and the scorched earth around this town has got my attention. I grew up in the city of Canberra as a younger kid, which some people call a 'country town'. Clearly, they've never been to Wirrulla.

This is the first place I've really stopped and asked myself: *what the hell am I doing?*

The reasons I left Aunt Cheryl's and Melbourne two days ago are still crazy in my head. I caught a train to Southern Cross Station, dropped my backpack on the concourse, and looked all around me. I thought something would stick out, or something would make sense? Maybe someone would come tell me what to do next?

No one did.

And in that moment—in all the noisy silence—Tony's words were hounding me like a mad dog growling and snapping at my heels.

'Get a real job,'

'Proper hard work is what you need, not bloody *computers*.'

Truth was, he didn't give a toss about me, I knew that. But occasionally, he'd get all heated-up about where I was headed. 'Stupid dreamer, you are. Thought you'd be a pilot.' He'd laugh. 'What happened there, ay? Nah, kid, this is where you'll live, work, drink, and die—just like me, and just like the rest of us. That's how the world works around here and you're nothing special.'

Nothing special?

I knew I had to shake free of it all. Had to get Tony's crappy voice right out of my head. I realised right there and then, I needed to get totally out of Melbourne. Aunt Cheryl had been right about that. So, I panicked and bought a ticket for the next bus going anywhere. Adelaide.

And from there, I wanted to get even further away from Melbourne. Western Australia seemed like the best idea—almost like I'd be going overseas, but not—so after I got off the overnight bus in Adelaide, I headed further west on foot and hitched as many rides as my thumb could get me.

What a dumb idea. No, what a *really dumb idea*. Walking in the dry heat with a heavy backpack and trying to manage my asthma was the last thing I should've done. I could've afforded a plane ticket, but no, I had to be all stupid like I needed to conserve cash.

I managed to hitch some good rides though, and the latest got me here to dusty old Wirrulla. Had a counter-meal in the hotel, two glasses of coke, and one for the road. The guy I hitched with was going on further to Ceduna, but he'd sunk way too many beers, so I said, "Thanks, mate," and left on foot.

Now I'm standing here under the veranda with no choice but to get walking and face the midday heat.

I don't get far before I notice a fancy campervan creeping along the street. I'd seen it before; it had pulled out of the car park behind the pub.

"Where are you headed?" comes this voice from the van.

"Ah, going west. Heading for Perth."

"Hop in." He motions me towards him. "It's your lucky day."

··········

Present day, Western Australia

Pothole sighs out a slow groan. "Don't tell me. That fella is the reason you took off solo in the middle of frickin nowhere."

There's his sixth sense again.

I can feel my face going red. "How'd you know?"

"Been around the blocks, I have, mate. Been around the blocks and seen me a lot 'a different people. Ain't nothin' surprises me anymore."

I blow out a big breath and raise my eyebrows. "Oh, I think this might."

"Go on then," he says. "Surprise me."

··········

O2

One day earlier, South Australia

So, I get into the fancy campervan and we drive through Ceduna and head across the Plain.

This bloke seems friendly enough. George is his name—a tall fella, and balding. Talks about himself a bit, until his conversation comes around to me. "So, Perth. What's waiting for you there?"

"Not much."

He laughs.

"Seeing where things take me," I add.

"Right. So, you're moving there?"

"Yeah, that's the plan."

"Looking for work?"

"Yep."

"What do you do?"

"I'm pretty good with IT, a bit of a jack-of-all-trades. I plan to make a go of that."

"Ah, well, Western Australia is the land of opportunity, mate. You're headed the right way."

"Cool."

George asks me lots more questions and I tell him a few things. Enough to shut him up. Nowhere near the truth.

···········

We're many k's out of Ceduna now, and every time I think this desert can't get any flatter, or dryer, or hotter—it does.

George has been quiet for a long while, and then he says, "You know, Dylan, things happen for a reason. It's not by accident we met up today."

"Yeah?" Not sure what this guy's deal is.

"Too right. Something told me I'd meet a nice young man today, and he'd need a bit of a helping hand. A bit of guidance." He pauses. "I reckon that must be you."

"Oh," I cough and straighten up in my seat.

This is all getting a bit … strange.

The van's left turn signal is blinking, and the speed is reducing. I thought we'd be sticking to the highway?

"Hang tight," he says. "Have you seen the Great Australian Bight?"

"Um … no."

"Like I said, it's your lucky day." He smiles hard as we take a left off the highway onto a gravel road.

My next words come out tight and squeaky, "Where are we going?"

"A quick detour. The coastline of the Great Australian Bight is not far away, and it's beautiful, you'll love it."

I look around and see no sign of the coast.

"I'm also headed for Perth," George says. "Stick with me. I'll take you all the way. And I have good connections there and a network of contacts. We'll find you some work."

"Oh, right."

This sight-seeing diversion might even be worth the bother? I think about it as we drive on. At least another ten kilometres. Could've been twenty. And still no coast.

My mouth's got dry and my breaths are short and hard. "Is it much further?" I blurt.

"Almost there." He looks at me with this cheesy smile. "It's all good, Dylan. You're fine with me." It's at that point his left hand comes off the steering wheel and rests on my right knee.

I flinch a bit. Can't help it. I can't even recall the last time Aunt Cheryl touched me like that.

He pats my knee a few times. "It's all good. Stick with George, you'll be fine."

Now I'm like … frozen.

What the hell? Something's way-off here—

"Nothing happens by chance," he says, patting my knee again. "We were meant to become friends today." It's at that point, his hand finishes further up my leg, on the edge of my shorts.

It's at that point, I lean towards him.

He turns and gives me a knowing grin.

Without looking, my right hand fumbles for the handbrake lever between our seats. I find it, and with both hands yank it upwards with everything I've got.

George snaps his eyes back to the road in horror. He yells as the vehicle swings left, then right. Stuff goes everywhere—paper, pens, a cup, a book. Stuff crashes in the back.

Now the van is stopped dead and as the dust clears, we're sitting full-on sideways across the road. George's knowing grin is gone, replaced with a great unknowing. He looks at me all wide-eyed like he's seen a demon.

Time to grab the passenger door handle and pull. I'm out of there before I decide to be out of there. I yank my backpack out, slam the door, and jog away. *Fast.*

I'm a good half-a-kilometre away before the sound of the campervan comes up behind me. It slows and the passenger window whirs down.

"Dylan, look, sorry mate. I didn't mean to—"

"Piss off. Pervert."

"Dylan, we—"

I slam the side of his van with a good hard swing of my backpack.

George's face changes again, big time. "Why the heck did you do that?" he yells.

"*Everything happens for a reason*, you reckon. You figure it out!"

The van roars and skids and leaves me in a cloud of orange dust.

....

Present day, Western Australia

"I can still taste it," I say.

"The dust?" Pothole asks.

"Yep."

"Damn bloody pedo. I got a fair idea what his *network* was. It went by a very well-known name back when I was a kid."

It seems like Pothole's got more to say on this subject, like he knows more. But I really don't want to go there.

"Right," I mumble.

"You don't wanna know about all my old crap. I can tell," Pothole says. "That's okay, I get it." He shifts in his seat and squints out at the road. "And you don't know me much, but I hope you can understand you're okay with me. I'm not like that George fella, not one bit."

"Yeah," I say, "I get that."

"Good." His relief obvious. "Took me a long time to trust anyone when I grew up. Way too long. Don't go and do what I did, Dylan.

No matter how shitty some people can be, when you come across people you can trust, stick with 'em. That's all I can say."

I nod, but I'm not really sure what he's on about.

"So, getting back to yesterday, after George-y-boy took off in a puff of dust. You was gonna walk back to the highway, was ya?"

"I had no choice. There was no one else out there, and zero phone reception too."

"Right, yeah. Then what happened?"

"Dunno. I remember running out of water pretty quick. It was so hot, and I walked on for frickin hours. Must've been over twenty-k's that road. I don't remember much afterwards."

"You was damn lucky. I'd gone off the highway to get some sleep. Ya might still be there, otherwise."

"Yeah."

"And your mate George; he was dead-wrong, you know."

"How's that?"

"There ain't no reason everything happens. You just got lucky, young fella."

I shake my head. "Lucky. Yep, that's me."

"You're a bit touchy about the luck thing, aren't ya?" he asks knowingly. "There's more to your story, that's for sure. But don't worry," he says, tapping the side of his nose with a finger, "I'm still keepin' me sticky nose outa all that business, yeah."

I shrug and swallow hard. "Yep."

Pothole drives on for a good while. He stays quiet, except for some ditsy old tune he whistles through missing teeth.

My mind works overtime, though. The damn thing will not shut up.

Luck?

There's so much Pothole doesn't know, thank god, but so much my mind won't let go.

"But I'm not going to just wait for luck to come my way," I suddenly blurt out, like an unexpected voice of wisdom from right out of nowhere. "I'm going to make things happen." I motion at the road ahead, my pointing finger held straight and hard. "*That's* why I'm headed for Perth."

Damn, so I'm thinking aloud now?

Pothole waves a hand slowly across the width of the windscreen, sweeping at the desert like some movie character dude about to launch into a big speech. "Ah yes, the great promised land," he says. "The land of milk and honey."

Um … righto then.

"Sounds like you got a bit of a plan, after all, young fella. You're not so aimless and on the run, huh?"

"You bet," I say with all the confidence I can pull.

He flicks a gear lever, then scratches his stubble. "Yep, running towards something can be a good thing. It's the other side of it you gotta watch for."

"Other side?" I half-ask with a hint of sarcasm. "I don't even think there is one."

"Yep." He nods slowly, "… there is. There's also running from something. We can deny, switch, and avoid our past all we like. But one day, the thing you run from is gonna come get ya." He scratches his beard. "Yep. I've been there, tried that."

I laugh at his words like a psycho. "*Hah*! Not me. Nope. I'm all good. Nothin' bad's in my rear-view."

Pothole takes a long careful look in his big side mirror like he's checking the road back there to see if I'm telling the truth. Then he looks right at me for a long second and gives me a pronounced nod. "Y…ep," is all he says.

I stare back at him, trying with every fibre I've got to communicate zero emotion, despite the weirdness now bubbling and bouncing around in my head.

Pothole leans sideways and presses some buttons on the dashboard. The dying geriatric cat starts up again through the truck's speakers. Old mate country singer was still missing his missus and happy to share more of his deep feelings.

This time, though, I'm not complaining. Maybe this country crap isn't that bad?

Now you're gonna leave me again,
And I won't say Amen,
Your tail lights got me sad,
So, darlin' … don't go … 'coz honey, I love you too bad.

Yeah, nah, scrub that. It definitely is.

I settle back in my seat, close my eyes, and try to concentrate on what might lie ahead. I'll forget the stuff behind me, and that's where it'll stay.

6

It's mid-morning as a big green sign flashes past on my side of the trailer cab: *PERTH 85 KM.*

The night had been a blur of black desert, headlights, taillights, and weird-as dreams. The truck had driven on and on, and on. We stopped a few times and I think Pothole caught some sleep somewhere.

"I'll be heading into Belmont to deliver this load," he says. "You want me to drop you somewhere?"

"I'll head for the city, I think."

"Right. There're buses you can get near the freeway. I'll drop ya there."

"Cool."

This trip's been good, but I'm kinda looking forward to being on my own again. I think.

He takes a swig from a tiny metal flask he keeps to hand. "And then what?"

I go to answer him and realise I don't have an answer.

He's laughing again. "Yer still working on that plan then, ay?"

"Reckon the plan for the next few days is … there is no plan."

"You're gonna be fine, young fella. She'll be right."

"Who says?"

"Pothole says."

I steal a grin as I stare out the side window. Pothole's been the right person at the right time on the right stretch of outback road to nowhere. I hope he's got my life prediction somewhere near right, 'coz god only knows where he gets his info.

··········

The midday sun is dazzling as I step out from the underground bus station in downtown Perth. The air is like an oven. People are everywhere—all going somewhere, all doing something. Important people doing important things.

But me? Nah. More the opposite.

There's a wide street going one way, a big shopping place straight ahead, and lots of shiny glass skyscrapers out in the other direction.

As I put one foot out to start walking, I'm smiling to myself again. The great unknown feels like it's all on me, but this new freedom is like the first hit from a drug I've never had. And yeah, I might look like a homeless loser to all these high-flyers walking past—that's if they even notice me—but things are going to be different. I know it.

But which direction should I go right now? Should I turn my foot left or right?

I snigger to myself. *No idea.*

I turn right.

"Hey, watch it," a woman with a briefcase snaps as she sidesteps around me. She's still glued to her phone as she charges off towards somewhere very important.

Whatever.

A glass skyscraper nearby has this swanky little eco-park at its base with some shade and a pond. Too good to resist in this mega heat, so I settle back against a low wall and think through what's next. Aunt Cheryl's note is still in my back pocket, like it's nagging me. I could find a backpacker's somewhere near the city, or I could call her number and see what happens?

The number wins in the end.

"Hello." I can tell straight away from the voice, the lady's pretty old.

"Ah, g'day. This is Dylan."

"Dylan who?"

"Dylan Malloy. My Aunt Cheryl gave me your number."

"Oh, Cheryl ... Cheryl Malloy, from Melbourne?"

"Yeah, yeah. That's her. I'm her nephew."

"Oh, I see." There's a long pause. "Well, what can I do for you, Dylan?"

"I'm ah, I'm here now, and looking for a place to stay for a bit. Cheryl said I should give you a buzz."

Her voice trailed off, "Did she? I see..."

Maybe Aunt Cheryl was wrong and the backpacker place should've won out?

··········

I caught an Uber out to the lady's place in Cannington, fifteen minutes from the city. She invited me over for a cuppa, and I had nothing else to do, so...

Now, I'm sitting here on this hard, antique-looking lounge with a tiny china cup and saucer in my hand. I've never had tea in my life, but ... anyway. It totally fits with the vibe of this old place, though.

All flowers and tidy garden-beds on the way in, timber front porch with fancy trims, big entry hall decorated with expensive stuff from centuries back. Fairly big and dark inside, but smells like … a home. And it's about twenty degrees cooler than out in the sun, unlike this goddam teacup.

Nancy is stirring her tea very slowly. "So, your Aunt Cheryl said you could stay here, did she?"

"Ah, not … exactly. She said if I ended up in Perth, you were an old friend of hers and I should get in contact. Like, you might be able to help me out at first, or something?"

"I see."

She's pretty hard to read and I'm not sure what to say next. Feels like I've invaded her space. But now that I'm here, this place feels kinda right. "I'll be looking for somewhere to stay, but I really don't want to impose—"

Her tea stirring suddenly stops and her eyes tighten. "*Nonsense*," she says. "Of course you will stay here. Cheryl was a good friend and any relative of hers is welcome here with me."

Didn't expect that.

"Oh, great, thank you. Thanks so much."

She seems trustworthy, but something tells me there's more to this lady.

Nancy places her teacup on a side table, carefully. "I won't have freeloaders, though," she says, matter-of-fact. "If you need to stay for more than a few days—for weeks or even longer—then you will need to pay board."

"Of course, yeah, no probs," I say, cool-as.

Nancy's voice is dead-flat, and her face gives me nothing. "And I do enjoy my peace and quiet, so I'd expect you to be out working during the day." She straightens and holds a knee tightly with hard-clenched hands. "This isn't a waiting area for dole claimants."

"Oh, yeah. No, I mean … I intend to work, for sure."

Nancy tenses and bites her bottom lip. "Do I gather then you've come here *without* an offer of employment?"

She's got me there. No job leads. No offers. No resume. Everything happened in such a rush in Melbourne, I didn't even bring my school results or a work reference. I only brought determination—bucket loads of it.

"You … could say that, yes," I reply, thinking how I can reassure her. "But I'll be out looking for work straight-up. No worries there. It's cool."

"Glad to hear it, young man." She stands and brushes down her dress. "Now, let me show you to your room."

Nancy swings open a door at the far end of the hallway. And jeez, what a room. Huge. High ceilings. Dark timber everywhere. The scent of dried flowers. Frilly windows with red and green stained-glass surrounds. A big double bed with posts, like the Queen might've stayed here.

"I hope you'll be comfortable," she says with a smile.

"I'm sure I—"

And then it starts.

Not now. Please, not now.

But it's no use. I cough and hack and splutter and say words of apology in between when I can. And it goes on and on for what feels like forever.

"My goodness me," Nancy says as she pats me on the back. "That is one very nasty cough. Are you ill?"

I drop my backpack to the floor and dismiss her question with the wave of a hand. "No, no. Just some dust from all the travelling, I think. Outback roads and all that."

She raises an eyebrow at me. I've never seen an eyebrow go that high. The angle is insane.

I want to deflect her; I hate it when people worry over this silly cough. "Have you heard from my Aunt Cheryl," I ask, "like, in the last few weeks?"

"People of your generation use the word *like* far too often, don't they?" She taps a finger on her cheek. "And oddly out-of-context, which is doubly irritating."

"I guess, like—"

She tuts. "And, no. I have not heard from Cheryl for a few years now."

"Oh."

Nancy tilts her head the other way as she reads my surprise. "Is there something the matter? Is Cheryl alright?"

Seems Nancy has some feel for the crappy side of Cheryl's life, minus the recent details.

"Oh, yes, yes," I lie. "She's cool."

Nancy leaves the room and I sit on the bed, put my head in my hands. Should I have told her? But how could I? I only met the lady half an hour ago and I can't just unload on her with all my crap. And besides, I'm in Perth now. This is the start of my new life.

But as Nancy disappears into the hallway, a thought is starting to dawn on me. This is the first time since Melbourne that I've really thought about what happened just before I left. I've been pushing it all down, but everything's still quite raw and it can't stay down there forever.

One week earlier, Melbourne

"Hey."

Aunt Cheryl's out at the clothesline, hanging up a load—hi-vis and oversized undies everywhere. "Hi," she says, without turning.

She likes to talk when I get home from work. But not so much today.

So I start the chat, "Whazzup?"

She shrugs. "Same old."

"You want a hand with that?" I say, as I pull a pair of wet jeans out of the basket.

"Leave it."

Huh?

I don't get it. I've been trying to help more around here—do my part. Been working casual for a local computer business since finishing school and it's been good to earn some cash. I slip Aunt Cheryl a fifty when I can to help her out.

I ignore her and hang the jeans anyway, then pull a t-shirt from the basket and move to an empty spot on the line.

Cheryl stays in the same spot and twists herself sideways. The clothesline turns, and a pillowcase comes between me and her. But there's no hiding what I saw. There's no hiding the thick swelling on her cheekbone and the dark bruise above it. And there's no hiding the white bandage behind her ear.

I spin the clothesline the other way and step toward her. "What the hell?"

She twists further away and uses a hand to cover her cheek and ear. Her head drops and her eyes close.

"How did you get that?" I point at her bruise.

"It's nothing. I fell, that's all."

I was as surprised by my next sentence as she seemed to be. "This was Tony, wasn't it?"

She stood there like a statue, stared into space, and said nothing.

I'd suspected it for a while. For too long. Sometimes she'd have a limp, or a stiff arm, or she'd wince when she lifted something, like her ribs hurt, then try to hide it.

Tony is an utter cockhead, no doubt there. But he's not stupid. He'd been hurting her where the injuries don't show. I was working it out, but I'd been too afraid to say anything.

I say, "You fell into one of Tony's fists, didn't you?"

She shakes her head and stares at her feet.

"That prick's going to get what he deserves, I—"

"No Dylan. *No.*" And she points a finger at me, hard. "Stay out of it."

"This can't keep happening. I know it's not the first time, is it?"

That question—my question—grips my guts. All those other times are rolling back through my head. Those other times I heard things, saw things, sensed things, but chickened out. I'd just shut my bedroom door. I'd whack on my headphones and listen to a thrash-metal banger full bore. I'd take off and not come back for hours. And I'd think about my mum and what coulda been, and how things are, and about this hellish place I somehow ended up at. And I'd block Aunt Cheryl out of my head. I'd freeze any thoughts of Tony throwing stuff, or landing a slap, or letting a left hook fly. I'd lock it all out by only thinking about me.

How could I do that? What was I even thinking?

"Look," Aunt Cheryl pleads, "we can be hot-headed, us two, and we fight sometimes, and yell a bit."

I reply with my sarcasm level set to the max, "Oh, really? Gee, I never noticed."

"We pushed-n-shoved a bit, and I fell. That's all."

Her pretend giggles as she's talking aren't selling her story to me one bit. Does she think I'm still a fourteen-year-old kid?

"So, it's *your* fault?" I ask. One of my hands is up and pleading now. Pleading for her to cut this denial crap and talk to me straight. And for a microsecond I see myself there: head to one side, eyes wide, a hand up. Just how Mum would look.

Cheryl glares at me. "It's just the grog. When he sobers up, he'll regret it and be sorry. We'll make up. It'll be fine," she says, tugging at an earlobe like she wants it removed.

I'm not buying this. No way. So I ask, "Like last time?"

And now she goes all parent-ey on me and leans forward with one hand on a hip, "Leave it. *Please*," she barks, like I'm some little kid who should shut-the-hell-up. And she looks full-on as if she will not back down. Her face is red. She's dragging in quick, short breaths like she's just come off a marathon.

But I'm still not convinced. Her faked-on parenting act only tells me I'm on the right track with this.

We stare at each other for the next few seconds. Neither of us flinch.

I steady my breathing and tone things back. "I will, but only after you've done something."

There's more awkward silence until her curiosity takes over. "Done what?"

"Once you've called the cops and reported this."

She looks horrified, takes a step back. "No way. *No*. Don't be stupid, Dylan." She's struggling to maintain the sting and drive of her words. "You're over-reacting."

I take a step towards her. "If you don't call 'em, then I'm going to confront Tony myself. Your choice."

Aunt Cheryl turns away and stares into the distance—long past the endless rows of wobbly backyard fences, the rust-coated clotheslines, the grey-block garages, and corrugated sheds. Past the boundary of this suburban hellhole, and the next, like she can see in her imagination a horizon out beyond the city. And she whispers now. She whispers to me, but more-so, to herself. "You can't fix this. There's ... there's no way out."

An instinct is building inside me. Something foreign. Like a volcano about to go off. This raging impulse to protect. An urge to defend, regardless of any danger. And an unfamiliar sense I should hold her in my arms and tell her everything's going to be okay. But my feet don't move—stuck to the spot by yet another instinct I don't understand.

"We'll find a way," I say with all the pretend confidence I can generate. I may not know what to do here, but I am not letting it go. Not this time.

Aunt Cheryl's gaze returns from the far distance. She stares into my eyes like she's trying to find something in her head to say, or do, but can't.

••••••••••••

It's late afternoon the next day as I come up the driveway. Should I be relieved or disappointed to see Tony's car is not here? Dunno. I've got no real idea what's going to happen in the next few hours, but whatever's going down, I just want this *done*.

Aunt Cheryl is sitting on her own in the kitchen with this look on her face like she's just binged the most extreme horror series ever. A huge suitcase and two bags are plonked near the back door.

I look at the bags. Look at her. This was not what I was expecting. I swallow hard. "What's up?"

She finishes something on her phone and points at the dining table. "Sit down."

I pull out a chair and sit uneasy on the front edge as if I don't want to be there, like I'm primed and ready to bolt.

Aunt Cheryl takes a deep breath and clasps her hands on the table. "Things have changed, Dylan. I need to tell you what's happening."

"Right."

"I couldn't risk you confronting Tony. He would do you serious damage."

Damage? That loser can hit women, yeah, but if he tried it on me *I'd cave his frickin head in.*

I clench a fist, plonk it on the table, and straighten. "I could deal—"

"Shut up and listen," she says. Aunt Cheryl looks like she's shocked herself. "He'd hurt you, believe me. I promised your mother I'd take care of you, and that's what I'm doing."

"Doing?"

"The years since … since what happened have been tough, but I've wanted you here the whole time," she says. Her voice softens as she stares at her clenched hands, "You're growing up into a really good young man I'm proud of." Now she swallows and blinks. "You mean a lot to me, Dylan, and I want you to have the very best life. I just know, given half-a-chance, you're going to make something of yourself. You can be somebody—away from here," she says, flicking her hand across the table surface.

Dunno what to say. It sounds like she's throwing me out, but no, she wouldn't…

She looks up now, into my eyes. "It's not safe for you here anymore. You've got to get out of this hellhole and make a break for it. Get clear of all this and get on with your life."

I lean back, grip my head either side, and hold my breath. I don't understand. Get out of here? Get on with my life? How? Where?

"You don't want me here?"

"Of course, I do." Her voice catches. "It's not that simple. I have to do what is best for you."

I don't get it. How is it best for me to leave and be on my own? And who'll be here to protect Aunt Cheryl?

"But, what about you?" I ask.

"Don't worry about me, I'm not your responsibility."

I look up at her. Is she kidding me? "You're all I've got."

"I know," she says as her tears start. She swipes at her face and they stop almost as quick. "I've made arrangements with your mum's lawyer."

Cheryl hands me a business card and I take it from her in slow motion. I read the letters and words and numbers, but my mind takes none of it in.

"He's going to be the main trustee for your fund from now on, not me," she continues. "You've got an appointment with him tomorrow morning at nine. There's some money to transfer to your account for now, and he'll explain how you can access the rest of it down the track."

"I don't get it, I—"

She reaches across the table and takes one of my hands. "Look. There're points in life when things happen and you gotta take your chances. You can't see where it's leading, but you take the first step and you keep going. Take this chance, Dylan. Use what you've been given. Go and make a life for yourself."

"Go where?"

"Anywhere but here. If you stay, you'll get crushed. There's no future for you here, Dylan. Not in this place. Not in this house."

"But *you're* here?" I plead.

I want a chance to fix everything, to make things right. I want to put Tony in prison or in a coffin. I want Cheryl to be safe. And I want a chance to get myself together before I go hit the world on my own.

"I won't be," she says, deadpan. Her gaze switches across the room to the packed bags, and that's when I realise they are hers, not mine. Now, she's staring at the back wall like she's imagining the horizon out there again. "I'll be gone very soon … for good."

How can 'for good' be any *good*? My throat dries up and my feet are tingling. Am I here? Is this happening? It all seems way too surreal, and very final.

"Where?" is all I can whisper.

She leans over the table again and places her hands on mine, her grip firm. "Don't worry about that. I'll be okay, and I'll call you in a few weeks. This isn't a final goodbye, Dylan, it's just what's best for now."

I slump onto the table and hide my head with my arms.

"I did what you said, Dylan," she says. "You gave me no choice. I rang the cops. They've got Tony in custody now."

I lift my head. "For real?"

"Yes, for real, but he'll probably be out of lock-up by tomorrow afternoon." She stiffens and grips the edge of the dining table. "I'll be gone by then, Dylan. And so will you."

My head spins and I rock back in the chair like someone's upper-cut me.

Aunt Cheryl gets up, comes around behind me, and kisses the top of my head. "Pack your bags and take whatever you can. Take what you want from the house too. Just get to the lawyer's office by nine tomorrow and never, ever come back here."

The silence hangs between us as my mind goes into a full-on flat spin.

"You hear me?"

"Yes," I hear myself say.

But what does she even mean?

···········

When I come back into the kitchen a half-hour later, there's a folded note on the dining table with my name scribbled on the front.

The suitcase and bags near the back door are gone.

So is Aunt Cheryl.

7

Two months later, Perth

Shadows of tall city buildings are getting longer outside as the sun drops out past the coast. I'm feeling the pull of the great beyond—the world outside this little café tucked between all the skyscrapers in Perth's inner CBD.

My work here is casual and really basic. Taking orders, clearing tables, cleaning-up at the end of the day. It's easy and often gives me time to go over things in my head.

Sometimes I think back to Melbourne and all that happened there, but the place is fading in my memory. The faster it goes, the better. Aunt Cheryl calls me from a silent number every few weeks. Says she's moved to Tasmania and changed her last name. Tony got charged, pleaded guilty, and got off with good behaviour. He'll probably have another woman now, but at least he's not hurting Aunt Cheryl anymore. She told me not to say a word to Nancy about anything.

Okay, be paranoid, whatever.

And anyway, I've decided I like it here in Perth. The place has this fresh vibe about it. The sky is clear most days and the beaches are the best I've ever seen. It's often boiling, yeah, but not very humid. Pothole called it 'the land of milk and honey' or something, but Perth's more like the land of silk and money. There's so much going on here—big business, big dollars. Maybe that's what he meant.

Further time to get settled and look for the right IT job would have been better, but there's been no time for that. Not with Nancy breathing down my neck from day one. And steady cash from this job and from delivering pizzas at night means I can stay on with her and pay the board without having to dip further into my trust fund. I'd much rather live on my own, to be real, but I reckon her place is much cheaper and easier than a flat or a share-house.

"I'm done, boss. The cleaning's all finished," I say as I pull off my apron.

Max, the café owner, is crouched over his laptop and looks like his head will blow a fuse any second. "Huh?" he replies, not looking up.

"See you on Tuesday."

"Yep," he says, still glaring at the screen. His index fingers are banging the keyboard with real intensity.

The outside and freedom are calling as I reach for the door handle—

"*Argh*! Damn this," Max fumes.

I'm tempted to ease through the front door and away, but *no*. Maybe it's the boredom of working this hospitality job, but it's like something's steering me back to what I'm good at.

"What's up?" I nod at the laptop.

"My stress levels, that's what!" he says a bit too loudly. Then he turns toward me and throws both hands in the air. "This bloody tax website and all this ridiculous security and identity crap. How's anyone supposed to run a business in this country?"

"Like me to have a look?"

Did I just say that? *Yes you did, dickhead.* You should be outta here, but your stupid mouth's got you being a hero.

"Nah, it's well over your pay-grade, Dylan," Max says. "Thanks anyway."

"I'm, like, pretty good with software and all that."

Two years working casual for an IT fix-it company back in Melbourne taught me a heck-of-a-lot. I developed a thing for systems and business software and making them work, and I became one of the main go-to guys for difficult clients and tough computer problems.

I wander over to see a dialog box pop up on Max's screen with a cheerful ding:

YourGov has locked your account due to irregular activity. Please contact our help desk for assistance. Fatal error 40166.

Max rocks back in his chair and grabs his head with both hands. He kicks away with his feet and rolls away from the desk. His eyes are on the ceiling and his face is going deep crimson.

I wheel another chair over. "C'mon. Let's see if we can fix this." He doesn't know it yet, but Max's life-threatening IT issues should be a walk in the park for me.

Max's eyes come down and he turns towards me. His blank expression is telling me he thinks I'm dreaming. "You sure?"

"I'm sure."

He shrugs. "Got nothing to lose, I guess."

"Right, so talk me through what you were doing…"

…••••••…

The crimson has left Max's face, and he's even managed a laugh. It's taken us a couple of hours to get things sorted. He had duplicate identity accounts which confused the heck out of the government systems he was using. A few calls to help desks and software uninstalls-reinstalls got it all fixed. I got his accounting software working better too. No more manual uploads and keying-in figures. Just click a button and the activity statements get uploaded to where they need to be.

"Gawd, just like that?" His eyes look like they'll pop, but more with amazement than rage this time.

"Yeah." I push up off the chair and stretch; my body's not used to sitting at the keyboard for so long anymore. "The magic of the InterWebs."

"Thanks, Dylan. I didn't realise you had these other talents."

I haven't lost my edge, clearly, but I reckon this must all be pretty bizarre for Max. I can make a decent coffee, and I'm okay at taking orders and clearing tables, so he must be wondering what the hell I'm doing working here? Fair question, I guess.

I just grin and say, "No probs. And ah … about that pay-grade you mentioned?"

"Fair call," he laughs. "There'll be a tidy bonus for you in next week's pay."

……•·•……

"That's a hell 'a good news, bro," Toby says loudly into my ear. "Max is usually uptight with his cash." Toby is a cook at Max's café, and he invited me out with some of his mates.

I grin and yell back over the thumping doof-doof of the music, "Yeah, pretty cool."

The packed night club at Northbridge is pulsing like a live beast. Everyone's given over to the vibe like they're a part of some bigger organism. All swept-up in the music, the sticky late-night heat, the drinks they're sinking, and whatever else. I wonder if I am part of this thing.

Do I look like an outsider?

"Scull that," Toby yells. I look at the glass he's just plonked on the bench in front of me. I reckon that's number five now, but I've lost count. The liquid is clear and all innocent, like water. My first impulse is to ask him what it is, but that only makes the others laugh, so I throw this one down my hatch instead. It burns my throat with a sickening sweet and sour blend of something and then hits my head with a warm rush.

"Phew. Awesome," I say, shaking my head fast.

The others snort and hoot, and someone disappears into the heaving crowd to buy yet another round.

Toby leans in, looking puzzled. "So, with your dank tech skills, how come you're working tables in a café and doing Uber-eats?"

"Good question," I say, "Guess I'm just finding my feet, paying the bills for now. But I've got other plans."

"Cool." His eyes are glassy but he looks interested.

"And hey, thanks for the invite."

He grins. "No probs, man. Can't have you sittin' at home on a Friday night playing Warcraft or something."

"Absolutely," I say, trying to sound enthusiastic.

Truth is, it *is* good to be out, even if the nightclub scene puts me on edge. I don't even know what 'fun' is anymore, and this might help. And I don't mind if Toby and his mates think I'm a geek. I am one, to be real, and an IT career is where I'm headed. And they don't know it, but I haven't touched a simulator or an online multiplayer world or a VR headset, in years.

But, whatever. This is now.

From the other side of the bench, Liam cups a hand to his mouth and half-yells, "Targets acquired. Two o'clock. Ten metres."

I get his targeting lingo, but what is he on about? Anyway, at more like three o'clock and twelve metres, three girls are perched up against a dark wall with drinks in hand. All bare legs and arms. Plastered makeup. Plunging tops—their cleavages are like beacons in the dim that just have to be noticed. Barely concealed smiles. They're whispering to each other and looking our way.

Well spotted, Liam, well spotted. His radar is way better tuned than mine.

"C'mon on then, go plug in your USB," Liam says with a huge grin. He jags a thumb toward our targets.

Our group cracks-up, so I laugh along too. It's not until someone else punches me in the arm and says, "Those snacks got their ports free, IT guru, *go get 'em!*" that I realise they are meaning *me*. I'm meant to be the heat-seeking missile.

Me? Oh god.

These guys don't know me or my backstory. They wouldn't know I've only managed a few dates back in Melbourne, if you could call them that. More like tragedies. Awkward geek-ish interactions with girls which felt like duelling lightsabres for me, and god knows how it felt for them. And only one ended in a proper hook-up, and that began on the awkward side too. Since I've been in Perth, I haven't even tried.

"Hah! Maybe next time, guys." I try my best to look and sound cool as I slide off the stool, "I was just about to head off."

"C'mon bro, night's open," Toby says, grinning again.

"Hey, yeah. I just got some stuff happening. Gotta deal. You know how it is."

Liam says, "It's cool, man. Good to meet ya."

With high-fives and grip-shakes completed all round, I'm out the door and into the relative quiet of the main street outside. And now, finally, I can let this bloody cough out: the one I've been holding back, but only just, for what feels like hours. I couldn't let the guys see that. No one should, and no one will.

··········

A world in a toilet bowl? Seems like it's all there is, sometimes.

I'm gripping this big old bowl, head dangling in space, knees aching on the cold tiles, just waiting for the next heave at the pan like there's no tomorrow.

Knock, knock.

"Dylan?"

Knock, knock, knock.

"Dylan. Are you okay?" Nancy says.

I thought I'd done a good job of sneaking in all quiet, shoes off, the lot, but she must have been awake. She can get stroppy when I get in late. She's fussy like that, as if she's worried something bad's happened to me.

"It's all good, Mrs M," I say, loud enough to be heard through the closed door behind me. Wishing I'd locked the thing now.

Her muffled voice comes through again, "You don't sound very well. Are you sure you're alright?"

"Yes. It's all good. I'm fine," I lie.

She probably thinks I'm pissed and can't handle grog.

If only.

This is something else, and it's in my chest not my stomach. And there's no fix either way. The doctors can't fix a hangover and they can't fix my asthma either.

Nope. Just me and a toilet bowl.

I wait for her footsteps to shuffle off down the hallway, but all I hear is silence. What's she going to do now—charge-on in?

I wipe the green and yellow stuff off my face with loo paper and drop it in the bowl with all the rest. The sound of the loo flush will send her away.

•••••••••••

Nancy is up before me the next morning, like always. She hears me in the bathroom and gets the toast on for me. I always tell her not to, and then she always tells me not to be silly.

The last spread of butter is going on the second slice as I come into the kitchen. Her timing is spot-on, like always.

"Good morning," she says, handing me the plate of steaming toast.

"Hey!" I try to sound upbeat. "Thanks for the toast. But you don't have to, you know."

"Don't be silly."

The sun is streaming through the dining-room window as I trowel serious Vegemite smears on my first bit of toast. Nancy is lit by the sun and doing her usual routine in the kitchen. She's always dressed like she's got somewhere to go and the colours of her outfit totally match. And there's not a hair out of place.

I had two grandparents once, but I was too young to remember either of them. I have little idea what grandparents are like or what they're supposed to do, but I'm thinking my grandma might have been a bit like Nancy. Meh … maybe.

"I was worried about you … how you sounded last night," she says.

"Ah, yep … sorry about that." I take my first bite of toast. I'm not worried about it, so why should she be?

"Are you sure you are alright?"

"Yeah, yeah," I struggle to say and swallow at the same time, "I've had this cough thing since I was young. I've got asthma and sometimes get bronchitis and chest infections, but I'm okay for now. I get antibiotics when it gets bad."

"But your coughing fits are happening almost every night now."

Now that I think about it, she could be right, but the last thing I need is her on my case. "Ah, I don't think it's—"

"Yes it is. It's got worse."

She's been counting? "Ah well. I'll live," I say. "Sorry I'm waking you up like that."

"It's alright. I sleep light anyway." She brings me a cup of coffee, and I don't know why, but it's always in a certain cup and percolated with a dollop of cream and two sugars. "I think you should see a doctor."

"Been there, done that. Many times." I take another bite of toast. Maybe if I talk with my mouth full, she will let it drop. "It's always the same. Get another script, OD on antibiotics, do my puffer, blah, blah."

"So, why's it getting worse, then?"

She has a point, but I shrug and reach to sip my coffee. I'm over talking about this. My asthma is my problem. Hopefully, she gets it and will leave things there.

Or, *not.*

"Here are the details for a good GP I know." Her tone is flat as she hands me a sticky-note. "Please make an appointment. I'd take you myself, but as you know, I don't drive."

"Ah … okay."

There. I've been told. Maybe that's what grandparents do.

I've gotten on okay without grandparents, I guess, and now I'm doing just fine without my aunt as well. It's kind of ironic. The old guy in the truck said something about finding people you trust and sticking with them. He said nothing about what to do when those people piss off and leave you to it. I'll be fine, though. I'm cool on my own.

And then, *thwack!*

I picture her when I'm thinking those words. The vision appears on this screen in my head, the one I can't control. One of her hands is up and pleading. Her head tilts to the right and her eyes have rolled a bit. My mum had these eyes—soft and wide. They could see through anything and anyone. And they can see through my self-reassuring bullshit right now, even from the other side of another world.

8

I pack up his plate, cutlery, and napkins. "I'll clear these for you, How was your omelette?"

"Very good, thanks." The customer looks up from his phone. "Compliments to the cook."

He seems to be a regular, this guy. Comes in for breakfast now and then, and always takes this table near the front window in the sun.

I head for the kitchen. "I'll pass that on."

"It's Dylan, isn't it?"

I stop and look back. "Ah, yeah."

The guy puts down his oversized mobile and smiles at me. "G'day. Gavin's the name. Gavin Wright."

"G'day." I haven't got a clue who this bloke is, but there's something else familiar about him.

"We haven't met before, not properly."

"Oh, right, I think I've seen you in here a few times?"

"Yeah. I work a few blocks away. I come in to see the little bastard sometimes and grab some breakfast."

"Up yours, asshole," Max says as he glides past the table and heads for the back of the cafe. Obviously, they know each other. Maybe he's been coming in for years.

Gavin laughs and waves him away. "I hear some good things about you, Dylan."

Who's been talking? I haven't been here that long.

"Yeah?" I half-say, half-ask.

"Max tells me you got his computer and office all ship-shape over the last few weeks."

Grinning now. "Oh, yeah. That."

"From what Max says, you know your stuff."

Max glides past in the other direction. "Unlike you, dickhead."

"Ignore him," says Gavin with a grin. "You wouldn't know it, but the guy loves me."

Hmm. Do I laugh, or—?

Gavin pulls a chair out beside him and points at it. "Sit down for a tick." His words sound more like a command and less like a question.

"Okay," I glance around for Max. I guess it's okay. I park on the edge of the seat.

"Are you working full-time?"

"Nah. I'm casual here two or three days a week, and I do food delivery some nights."

"Reason I ask, we've got some casual work coming up at my office. Thought you might be interested."

"Oh, okay. What type of work?"

"Our Perth office has around forty staff. We're part of a bigger national outfit, but we need someone local for desktop support on our computers. Someone sharp to help us with installs, troubleshooting, that sort of thing."

I'm trying to keep a lid on my enthusiasm, but this sounds really cool. "I'm not all that qualified, but—"

He smiles and opens his hands. "Don't stress it. I'm more about results and getting the job done. Going by what Max tells me, you could be a good fit for us."

"Um…"

"Interested?"

Now there's a question. Is this one of those moments, one of those points in time where I can only see the next step in front? I am interested, for sure. It's probably a level above the IT work I'm used to, but might not be totally out of my reach. I'm still weighing up those points when I hear my mouth blurt out, "*Yeah.* I mean, yes. I am."

"Good." Gavin slaps a business card down in front of me. "Call my EA to make an appointment. We'll talk further soon."

"Awesome. Thank you."

Gavin shoves back his chair and walks out of the cafe. As I watch him disappear down the street among all the office workers and delivery people and high-flying execs hurrying off to their jobs and going this way and that, I'm wondering what just happened. A great IT job just came to me. I didn't even have to look.

I'm still sitting at the table and shaking my baffled head when Max comes past again.

"Don't worry about Gavin. He might come across like a big scary executive, but he's pretty harmless. He had a troubled childhood, you know."

"Oh?" What do you even say to that?

Max scratches his cheek. "I knew his parents."

"Yeah?"

"Yep," Max grins. "They were my parents too."

9

Four months later

Nancy was right. She always seems to be right, which irritates the heck outa me sometimes. My coughing at night is worse, and it's been getting me sometimes during the day as well. I can hide it most of the time at work. I've learned to grip and swallow. To hold it. To keep self-control over the impulse to hack and hurl from my chest.

If I can't control it, I whip into the bathroom and hope no one else is there. If someone is, I go for the disabled loo instead. I can get rid of my chest loads pretty quick, clean myself up, get my breath back, and get back to work without people noticing—I hope. They probably just think I take more craps than most people.

It's a pity the loos are out past reception, though.

"Hey, Dylan," Kimberley says as I go past reception, yet again. I'm doing my best to walk through like a ghost, but she's as observant as ever. Nothing in this office happens without her knowing. Reception is, like, her little planet. She's cool though. Her smile would make anyone's day. Pity about her boyfriend.

"Hey," I say, with a casual upward nod of my head. It's what I always say to her. If I say anything else, I reckon I'll make a dick of myself.

The rest of the people in the office are a pretty nice bunch, too. I was pissing myself the first day I came in for a chat with Gavin, but everyone was cool and they seemed desperate for help with their IT troubles. Gavin put me on a trial run for a few days, then offered me part-time work. It's increased week-by-week and now I'm close to full-time here.

"There's a call for you, from the Sydney office," Kimberley says. "Line four."

"Thanks." I head for the oversized cupboard I use as an IT room.

"Dylan. It's Tuân," the voice says on line four, blunt as a stump. It amazes me how people so good with electronic communications can be so crap at talking to humans. But maybe it's how I sound? Don't know.

I say, "Hi, Tuân."

"We've got some new hardware coming for you, via courier. Should be there tomorrow."

"Cool."

"It's a replacement switch unit for the LAN there. Nice rack. More capacity for the expansion and better network security."

"Right," I say, squirming in my seat. He's building up to something and thank god he can't see me on this call.

"You'll need to install it one night this week, after hours," he says, all matter-of-fact.

"Me?"

"Who else? Send me a DM when it arrives. I'll email you the LAN settings."

Far out. I know next-to-nothing about rack-mounted hardware switches. But, like much of what I've been doing around here, I'll do my research at home tonight and fake it at work tomorrow. The job gets done, and no one seems to know any different.

"Okay."

There's a click followed by a dial tone. My conversation with the head of Information Technology at *OAG Logistics Australia* was done.

Yes, nice talking to you too, Tuấn.

All the experience I picked up as a kid—all the time online and learning computerised systems on my own—I thought it'd all been a waste of time. But I could fake it as a virtual pilot and now I can fake it as an IT professional, and the difference is: they pay me to do this stuff.

Sweet.

··········

"Thanks," I say as I take the plate of toast from Nancy.

I've stopped telling her not to make me toast, and she's stopped telling me not to be silly. It's like we have an agreement to not state the obvious now. Like we're in some domestic routine. It must suck to be married.

"How did things go with Doctor Green?" she asks, not looking my way.

Bugger. It's been a month since she gave me the note. "Oh, yep ... okay," I say, keeping my eyes on the toast.

"Did she help you?"

I'm looking busy on my phone now, things to do. I don't need her doctor's help. I've got work to get on with and a career to chase, so I'm just not going there. Things are easier that way.

"Yep."

Minutes pass. Dishes get washed. Drawers get slid. Cupboards swing open and shut with a click and a thud, some louder than usual.

"When did you see her?"

My phone drops to the dining table and I turn to face her. "Is this, like, an interrogation or something?"

"No, no…" She looks surprised. "I just—"

"Thanks for the info, Mrs M, but I'll deal with it from here."

There. That'll close the subject.

Nancy puts down her dish-towel, folds it neatly, then looks at me. "Really, Dylan? By not even making an appointment?"

"*Far out*, you're not my mother!" Those words and the fury embedded in them take me by surprise.

But not Nancy, it seems, as she takes a step towards me. "No," she blurts out all defiant, and then drops it down a notch, "but I'm sure your mother would say precisely the same thing."

My self-control is out the window now. She's going to cop everything she deserves. "Oh yeah, and why's that?" I half-yell.

"Because she cares about you."

"No, she doesn't, to be real."

Nancy stares at me and gulps like she's driven into a cul-de-sac at a hundred-k's. She steps back. "Oh, I'm sure she—"

"*Bullshit*. My mum is dead," I spit, shoving back my chair. "There's no care coming from a bloody grave is there?"

I head for Nancy's front door. I've had about enough of this place. I've had a gutful of being told what to do about my health. I don't need some meddling old woman pretending she's my mother. No frickin way.

"Dylan, *wait*!"

I stop automatically and instantly wish I hadn't. "What?" I groan.

"I'm very sorry. I didn't know."

A shrug is all I've got.

Silence, now, long and awkward. I'm still facing the front door.

"It helps explains some things, though."

Another shrug, and sharper this time. I'm short of breath, so I try to inhale a big one.

Nancy's voice is softer now, but she keeps at it. "Explains why you keep people out, and why you try to handle everything on your own."

I half-laugh, half-cough. "Oh, okay, so it's *me*, is it?"

"Look. Things happen, but you can't deal with every single thing on your own," she says. "That's not the way humans beings are meant to function."

I look at the floor. My eyes follow the zig-zags on the Persian hall rug, all going everywhere but nowhere. "Yeah, well, it's not me that makes stuff happen."

"That's not what I—"

I turn and eyeball her. "My life has been one damn thing after another so far. I'm not asking for it. Stuff just happens. People are there and then they leave and there's nothin' I do to make it happen, and there's nothing I can do to stop it happening, either."

"Maybe. But if you can at least take control of your own health, then why don't you? Why not get the right help?"

She just doesn't get it. I put my hands up like an agro cop in traffic. "*Whatever!*"

Nancy's eyes go like slits. "Stop acting the victim, Dylan. Yes, life can be hard. And yes, you can't control much of it, or other people or what they do, either. But if you don't take charge of your life where you can, if you don't take control when those opportunities are put right in front of you, well … you're asking for more trouble, aren't you?"

"I don't need more doctors. I'll manage fine on my own."

"Really? Take it from me, from someone who's lived her life and made mistakes." Her hands go on her hips now and she straightens. "*No. You. Can't.*"

Squint. Take another breath. Huff it out.

Think.

Nothing comes. But I know there's safety outside. Safety and fresh air and solitude.

My cough hits me again as I twist the door handle and bolt for anywhere but here.

10

Nancy's sticky-note about the doctor has been hanging there on my workstation for two months, all loud and fluoro and begging for my attention. Should've chucked it out by now, but I might have to call the number one day if things get much worse. My cough has been getting to me more and more and it's harder to conceal. I can't deny that reality anymore, not even to myself. But I'll just do what's necessary to keep working with no one noticing. Nothing's getting in the way of me doing this job, not even this … this whatever it is.

The trouble with Nancy's note, though, is it reminds me why we aren't talking much. Things are pretty low-temp at her place since we had the big argument, and our conversations are super-short and only cover the bare minimum. We're like ships in the night in daylight hours.

"Dylan. Got a sec?"

I swivel my chair towards the voice. "Hey, Mr Wright. Sure."

"For the hundredth time, call me *Gavin*."

"Sorry. Gavin, yep, got it."

He plonks himself on a nearby desk. "You're doing good work here, Dylan," he begins, "but my instincts tell me there's more to you than meets the eye."

"Oh?"

This could be interesting…

"You've fitted right in since you've started here. The right guy at the right time for the right job."

"Thanks. Yeah, this is the sort of work I want to do."

Gavin cocks his head sideways and his left eye squints. "Is it, though?"

What does he mean? I thought this was going well.

"Ah, yeah. I ah—"

"Tell me, where are you headed career-wise? What's your end-goal?"

Wow.

I scratch my head and take in a sharp breath. "IT just seems to fit me like a glove. I like the challenge. It's good to be fixing things and helping people."

"And you provide great support, Dylan. But is this your limit—your goal—working in IT support?"

My mind scrambles. Where is this going? Does he … know? And I think back to what Nancy said about taking control.

"To be honest, no," I say, feeling the anxiety surge in my stomach. I push on. "I want to go somewhere and make a difference. I want to, like … expand my skills and create things. I want to take the lead eventually, and really be someone."

Gulp. I can't believe I said those words.

Gavin doesn't shift from his laid-back slouch on the desk and his face and eyes hold steady, right at me. His gaze isn't hard or uncomfortable, though, even when he holds it for a few seconds without saying a word.

"Yep. That's what I figured," he says. "Some people are great at support roles and that's where they stay, which is fine, but I don't think that's *you*, Dylan. It's good to hear you want more."

I feel myself relax. "Yeah. I hope I don't come across like some smart arse, or anything."

"Nope. Don't be afraid of stating what you want and going for it."

"Okay."

Wow. Maybe I should try doing this more often.

Gavin grins. "Max was a bit pissed-off with me after I stole you from his café, but he's glad you're doing well here, and he'll get over it. It's ironic, though, because I might have to do the same."

I feel my eyes going wide and my mouth dropping. *What's happening?*

"I'm going to level with you." He steeples his hands and puts his elbows on his knees, leaning towards me. "Thing is, a higher-level IT position has come up in our Karratha office, out-of-the-blue. We could really use someone with your skills up there for a while. It'll still involve some support work, but there'll be opportunities to do more, if you play your cards right."

"Wow," I blurt. "Sounds cool. But … where's Karratha?"

Gavin slaps his knee and laughs. "Hah! It's our field office for oil and gas projects in the Pilbara, way up north. We've got a big team up there and lots of work going on. It's remote and hot up that way, but the money's good and it's the sort of place where you can get somewhere if you work hard. I think it'd be a good fit for you, and might lead to other things."

Other things? I'm liking the sound of this. "Awesome," I say. "Um, for how long?"

"About three months, we reckon. Until they find someone permanent."

Can I do this? Should I?

I faked things as their IT guy in the Perth office when I needed to, and lately I've become good enough at my job to leave the faking part behind. So, if that's what this Karratha position needed at first, well, I've been there, done that.

I have no idea what living and working in Karratha is going to be like, mind you, but it's a long way from Perth and might do me just fine right now. Things with Nancy have got to the point where I need to move on. She sure as hell isn't my mother and not even my relative, but she kept telling me what to do more and more until it all blew up. And now the cold treatment with her is doing my head in. A complete break with time on my own sounds like the real deal.

"Okay," I say. "Thanks for the opportunity, Gavin. Can I think about it for a few days?"

He winks at me and hops off the desk. "Sure thing. I've already recommended you for the position, but let me know by Friday."

·········

"I think your mind is already made up," Aunt Cheryl's voice says in my ear.

I called her to catch-up, as we sometimes do, but it was her opinion about the Karratha thing I really wanted to know.

"You think so?"

"Look. This is what you really want to do, isn't it? Why not take the plunge?"

"I guess."

"Is there something holding you back?" She giggles. "Don't tell me, you got a *girlfriend* in Perth, haven't you?"

"*Hah,*" I laugh. "Nah, no luck there. Nope."

"So, you're free as a bird, then."

There's a pause on the line as her words play through my head. And actually, there is nothing to hold me back. I'd be mad to let this opportunity slip…

"Yeah, you're right. And it's been good staying with Nancy and all, but she's starting to piss me off to be honest. I'm ready to move on from there."

Cheryl quizzes me further and I tell her how things have gone down at Nancy's.

"Nancy is a good person, you know. She can be abrupt, but she has a really kind heart. And anyway, I'd be saying the same sorta things to you. You should definitely see a goddamn doctor before you go moving to the outback. God knows what services they have out there for asthmatics."

"Yeah, yeah," I say.

"And Nancy has her own story, too. There are reasons why she might be over-bossy with you."

"*Reasons*?" I huff. "Whatever."

"It's not all about you, Dylan," Cheryl says suddenly. There's a long pause on the line before her voice gets even more serious. "You wouldn't know this, but Nancy only had one child—a boy. He was killed in a car crash many years ago, he'd been joy-riding with his mates. Just nineteen he was. Nancy still blames herself for it, I think."

"Oh…"

Now I feel like a right loser.

••••••••••

Aunt Cheryl was right. My mind was already made up. And even if it wasn't, the things she'd told me about Nancy—the whole thing about losing her son—only confirmed it was time for me to move on. I feel sorry for Nancy, yeah, but I just can't deal with it all. And I'm not her other son.

Five days later, things are getting real…

"Okay, Mr Malloy," Kimberley says with that super-cheeky smile of hers, "you can either fly up on Tuesday departing at five-thirty in the morning, or Wednesday leaving at two in the afternoon. Which would you prefer?"

I'm leaning all cool and casual on the reception counter until I hear the word, *fly*. My next words sound anything but cool. "Fly up?"

"Ah, yes." She wobbles her head like she's talking to a dumb alien. "That's what planes do. You know … wings, jet engines, hot pilots in uniforms, all that stuff."

If only she knew?

And with no control whatsoever, my stupid male brains spin away, yet again…

I'm sitting all cool and in charge in this large padded seat—sheepskin lined. Instruments, buttons, switches, flight controls surround me. I'm wearing a crisp white shirt. Four gold bars decorate each shoulder. Headset on. A cheesy grin as I casually press a button, then turn to face her.

And Kimberley? Her office outfit has transformed into a flight-attendant uniform. Tight. Short. Her hair and makeup are beyond perfect. And she's beaming a cheesy smile right back at me, eyes sparkling like runway lights. "Here you are, Senior Check and Training Captain and Chief Pilot—Captain Malloy," she says, as she hands me a coffee cup, then winks, "I made it extra hot, just how you like it, Dylan…"

"Dylan?"

The vision vanishes as quick as it came. I hate it when this happens. Why can't I control my own frickin head? All of that nonsense is supposed to be completely *gone*.

Anyway, back to reality. I brace myself on the reception counter like I'm about to skydive with no parachute. "Oh, sorry. Yep?"

She blinks. "About flying up … you were saying?"

I fake a laugh, then swallow hard. "Yeah, about that. Umm … I'd rather … not."

Kimberley looks again at her computer screen, her brow furrowing. "So, you'd rather go another day, or on the weekend?"

"No, no." *Please don't make me say this.* "I mean, I'd rather travel by bus or train or whatever, if that's okay."

She looks up at me like I don't understand. "It's okay. You don't need to save us money, Dylan. The company's got this all covered and we'll freight your belongings up separately."

I straighten up. "Thanks. Yeah, it's not that. It's just, like … something else."

Her face goes blank, and I can see her brain ticking away. *Loser*, she must be thinking. *Silly geek, weirdo loser.*

And no sign at all of her flight attendant uniform.

I desperately want to give her a clever excuse which'd get me back in her non-loser books, but nothing comes. And I can't tell her the real reason. I've never told anybody that. Some things are best left unsaid and locked in the past. Life's easier that way.

"Righto," she says, raising her eyebrows even more. "I'll see what I can do."

11

Two years later

'Yes,' I'd said to Gavin, let's go to Karratha for a while, wherever that is.

'About three months,' Gavin had said.

Three months? *Yeah, right.*

A day-and-a-half into the non-stop bus trip from Perth, I'd figured out Kimberley hadn't been thinking I was a loser after all. She'd given me a 'you've gotta be kidding' look. It'd made sense as I stared out at the endless flat West Australian outback from the bus window. The scenery changed little once we got into the real desert, kilometre after kilometre—all fifteen hundred of them, to be exact.

The dirt gradually changed from an orange colour to a much deeper shade as the bus approached Carnarvon, then to a red, and then even deeper as we got closer to Karratha. The rocks and dirt are coloured like rust you'd see on a burnt-out car dumped long ago. It's no wonder there's so much mining up here, the minerals are practically oozing out of the ground.

There were some bizarre road-signs along the way which broke the boredom at least. They pointed to mysterious places like

Monkey Mia, Exmouth, Manilya. We crossed plenty of bridges, too, but never a river, just dried-up creek beds going nowhere. Lots of indigenous-sounding places as well: Nanutarra, Pannawonica, Talandji, and on and on. It seemed like I was moving into a different time and a different world.

And as the bus had finally rolled into the outskirts of Karratha—after waiting for a minerals train that took what felt like an hour to cross the road—I remember thinking, *Oh my god, what have I done*? There's industry everywhere. Pipes, sheds, fences, warehouses, roads, wires, towers. Huge salt-pans, docks, and cargo ships out on the nearby coast. This place is made for work, that's for sure.

It was a relief when downtown Karratha appeared; a small modern oasis in all the surrounding desert and infrastructure, just minus the palm trees. As I stepped off the bus, it was like coming out of a fridge and straight into an oven. This wall of hot dry air hit me in the face and the pavement was like floor heating on steroids. Couldn't wait to grab my backpack from the bus driver and bolt for some shade.

"G'day, mate. Where's the best place to eat around here on a Friday night?" I asked a hi-vis-covered local who'd just stepped out of the post office.

He looked me up and down, smirked, then pointed to a street behind me and grunted, "The Tav."

"Ah ... thanks. What should I be looking for?"

"Oh, you'll know it when you see it," he said.

I'd found the place, eventually, after nearly melting into the footpath on the way and my phone auto-shutting-down before it self-cooked. Stumbled into the sports bar and dropped my backpack—sweating, panting, and desperately trying not to cough.

The place went instantly dead-quiet and everyone turned to look, like I'd appeared on the planet *Tatooine* in some Star Wars flick. It was horribly quiet for a few seconds until a big guy with a bushy beard yelled, "Someone give this boy a drink, he's half-fuckin dead!" At which point, the bar erupted in *yahoos* and *he-haws* before everyone turned back around and got on with their socialising. I got the feeling this was the way most newbies were inducted into Karratha.

I made it to the only empty barstool and tried my best to stay low and blend in.

Yeah, right.

"You're not from around 'ere, ay?" the girl behind the bar yelled across at me.

"Ah, nope. How'd you guess?"

"Pour that neck oil down ya cake hole, it's on the house." She grinned and slammed something big onto the counter with amber liquid spilling and sloshing onto the bar towel.

I was quickly learning how the scale of things here is very, very different. The jug of beer she'd given me was more like a bucket. Her boobs were massive and I was trying not to notice, but failing. The blokes sitting around me looked like battle tanks in blue tank top camouflage. The conversations were super-loud. The air cooled but sweaty. Music hard and heavy.

And then there was … me.

Still, somehow, I started to like the place, even from that unsettling first moment. And after two years of living up here, I still have a laugh when I think about the move and the first day. But, I'm pretty much a local now. There aren't many of us living here permanently, and most of the population at any one time are the unhardened FIFOs—the fly-in, fly-out workers who all dread getting here and then can't wait to leave. They spend two weeks working here in hell, then two weeks living it up in heaven—Perth, that is—and then repeat endlessly until a rich early retirement, or insanity, whichever comes first.

It can be hilarious seeing those newbie FIFOs get used to the place, too. They use the hot water tap just the once before they realise the cold tap runs at around thirty-degrees most of the year. Cold showers don't really exist. And they only drink the bore water once before they understand it's got enough calcium to sink a ship, and it gives them the shits—literally. Washing's great here though. It dries in thirty minutes flat, unless it's a rare, rainy day which gives your jocks-n-socks the equivalent of two-hundred rinse cycles in an hour.

Funnily enough, though, despite this place being like another planet, I've come to fit in quite well.

Well, mostly…

••••••••••

"Look out, *Varanus alert*!" Greg says, loud and clear.

Our Karratha office is this big two-storey concrete structure in an industrial area near the port. Project managers, engineers, technicians, and logistics people come and go here all the time. Around fifty people use the place, but the faces change daily. Many of our staff are out on oil and gas platforms all over the ocean near here.

Greg's a petroleum geologist who processes masses of exploration data and recommends things. But he's not out in the field today; he's here in the office to avoid fieldwork and being outside, like he often does.

My desk is near his, which is okay because he often has high-end IT needs. But it's also bad because Greg thinks he's a comedian. And true to form, he runs over to the big free-standing fan sitting in the corner. He sets it to the highest setting and turns the stream of air towards the door leading to the corridor. "I got this," he proclaims to everyone on the floor.

A few of the staff snigger and shake their heads, but most ignore him. They've been here, seen this.

Greg doesn't hang around for the expected applause for once. He heads out the back to the lunch room.

The *Varanus* thing used to get to me. It's a nickname Greg gave me. Varanus is the name of a small offshore island near here. It's a central hub where oil and gas is pumped from surrounding platforms and sent to the mainland for processing. They had a big explosion there ten years ago when a primary gas line ruptured. It was a big deal back then.

Greg started calling me *Varanus* when I started having more gastric trouble. Every week I was having these monumental diarrhoea events. The gas and smells with it were out of this world. Then it started increasing to two or three times a week and I couldn't always do the deed at a loo outside of the office. So it wasn't long before my personal gas explosions were getting noticed. A few of the guys made the connection to me and their gossip started doing the rounds. My nickname came soon after, all thanks to the local comedian, Greg.

A *Varanus alert* from Greg warns my colleagues not to go anywhere near the upstairs loos for a good half-hour. Awkward, but necessary, much as I hate to admit.

As Greg disappears around the corner, Allison Brambilla, or Allie as she's called, comes over from the other side of the office. She picks up the fan with one hand, moves it real close to Greg's desk and twists the fan-disc around to face it. She marches off muttering, "Dickhead," as she goes.

And she's getting a better reaction from the office crowd too. Plenty of laughs, smiles, and even some applause.

I'd applaud too if I wasn't cowering behind my computer monitor, pretending not to notice.

....

"Dylan, mate. Grab a seat."

Alan Piper is the field manager here and a good bloke. It's no big deal getting called to his office. The experience is more like a mate inviting you to the pub for a chat and a beer, but minus the beer. Alan's got a nickname, too. *Alpha* they call him. It's borrowed from the Piper Alpha oil platform disaster in the North Sea years ago. Insulting nicknames are how it goes around here and even Alan doesn't seem to mind.

"I wanted to talk to you about the new project app," he says.

"Alpha-One?"

"Yeah. You named it after me, didn't you?" he says, laughing.

I relax back in my chair. "Dream on," I say with a grin.

"Haha! Anyway, the guys testing it in the field on their iPads reckon it's the real deal."

This was good news. I'd spent the first year in the Karratha office getting their IT ship-shape. They were running a monstrous home network with horrible old gear and a dogs breakfast of computers and devices. The place was like a museum of how not to run IT from the last decade. Once we centralised and modernised all the gear, I played more with coding, databases, and apps. I've started streamlining workflows and the Alpha One app is my latest tool to support our project managers in the field.

"Cool," I say, trying not to grin but failing miserably.

"Pete reckons there's lots more scope for apps like these. He wants you to spend a few days with him out on the Halyard platform, to look at the possibilities."

The very thought of this opportunity should give me an instant hit of happy feelings, but instead I get this twisting, sickening sensation of dread in my guts.

"Oh," is all I can manage.

Alan pauses, attempts to reads my face, then gives up. "What?" he asks.

"Pete wants me out there, like … on the platform?"

"Yeah. He wants to get you more hands-on with how they work out there."

I bite my bottom lip. "Right."

Alan tilts his head. "Your enthusiasm knows no bounds."

I raise my eyebrows and scratch my neck. I look outside, look at the ceiling. Is there a way out of this?

"Would this be your first time out on a rig?" Alan asks.

"Um, yep."

"There's nothing to worry about. They'll keep you safe out there."

"Yeah, yeah. I know."

He taps his fingers. "Sounds like there's a *but* in there, Dylan?"

He's right. There's a major 'but' looming. I can't avoid asking the question. "But, how would I get out there?"

"Same as everyone else, mate, on a chopper."

I swallow hard and my hands go stiff. "I … I can't."

Now, Alan's head tilts the other way. "What's the matter?"

Not just dread now. Panic. Real panic.

"Um, I can't do that."

"You don't like flying?"

"Something like that."

"C'mon, mate, she'll be right. It's only a short hop, and there's never been a—"

And I hear myself interrupt and say, "Sorry. No. I just can't do it."

·········

The thought hits me even harder as I head back upstairs: this was the first time I'd ever fully said *no* to anyone here. I pride myself on being super-helpful and positive about solving things. Nothing's too hard for me, which is probably why no-one's ever asked if I wanted to return to the Perth office. They really want me here. In fact, they *need* me here. I'm really getting somewhere and making a difference, but now I've let someone down and that someone is the boss.

Yeah, great work, Dylan.

Greg's also heading for his desk as I come back through the door. He's whistling and stirring his coffee in time with his steps, but now he's stopped and his mouth is half-open. Greg turns and does a full three-sixty visual scan across the open plan office, looking at every single colleague in turn.

But everyone is heads-down and not looking his way.

Nothing to see here, Greg.

His desk is a mess at the best of times. Papers, print-outs, takeaway wrappers, empty chip packets, and disposable cups are piled up. I don't understand how he can work in all the chaos. But the big fan has done the trick. The top of his desk has appeared from under the chaos like magic and it looks completely clear for the first time. The floor around his desk hasn't fared so well, though. It's now full-on hectic.

Greg steps over his rubble, sits down like he's in a daze, and doesn't say a word.

A chat notification dings on my PC as I get back to my desk.

Allie: I forgot to give him an Allie alert :)

Her desk is visible from here, *just*, so I turn to look at her, without making it too obvious.

Allie's got this dark vibe going: straight black hair, deep eyes, and chiselled olive skin. Not goth or emo, more Euro. Fairly attractive, but seems broody too. I don't think I've ever seen her smile. She looks serious no matter what's happening, and she doesn't say much. Guess it comes with being an engineer.

And her face is no different right now, except she gives me the quickest of winks before she goes head-down again to something she's reading. But, even from here, her mouth looks to be held tight and her lips are turned up at one end.

I'm probably seeing things?

Yeah, maybe.

12

Three months later

"As I said, the tests were inconclusive."

"Yeah, I heard you." I lean forward. "But something's still not right with me."

Doctor Wickramasinghe looks up from the report and almost sings his words in a thick Sri Lankan accent, "There is nothing further I can prescribe for you at this time."

"What, so, I just have to put up with it then?"

He does big circles with his hands. "What I mean is—"

"Mate, if you were dropping sticky bombs out your backside like I do most days, I reckon you'd have a different opinion. I just need something to set me right so this stuff doesn't interrupt my work, nothing more, nothing less. Some pills, a potion, whatever. I just want this mystery thing fixed. Okay?"

Doctor Wickramasinghe takes in a deep breath, deflates back into his chair, and flips his fancy pen onto his desk. It bounces off my report and hits his coffee cup with a clang.

Has he given up on me?

"Some people reckon their poo doesn't stink," I say, "but I reckon mine stinks more than most."

"I have no diagnosis and therefore no 'fixes' for you," the doctor says while making air quotes with two fingers. "We cannot do anything further for you here, other than refer you to a gastroenterologist."

I know what that means—the Big Smoke—and there's no way I'm up for the bus trip from hell in this state. I half-turn away and cross my arms. "I can't go to Perth, not all that way for a ten-minute appointment."

"Very well then." He slides my test report back into a folder. That's it, he's done.

What's with this guy?

"I'm not making this stuff up," I protest.

"This is not for me to determine," he says, not even blinking.

"Oh. So you think I might be?"

He closes the folder and strides over to the door. "Good day, Mr Malloy," he says as he pulls it open. "Please see the receptionist on your way out."

Wherever he did his medical training, I bet he bombed out on bedside manner. That's why he ended up here as a GP out the back of nowhere.

Prick.

••••••••••

My gastro issues are front and centre, no matter what those goddamn tests say. The gut pains are real and my cough's getting worse. It's like this constant irritation all the time and every few days it feels like my lungs are filling with stuff. It's hard to get my breath sometimes.

Alan points to a chair. "Dylan, mate, grab a seat."

Back in Alpha's office. Time for another heart-to-heart with the boss?

He eyes me hard over the top of his specs. "Look. I don't wanna stick my nose in your business, but something's up. You don't seem right."

I shuffle in my chair. "Yeah," is all I manage.

"And you're here less and less."

"Sorry about that, I can—"

Alan puts up a hand. "Nah, mate. That's not the issue. You work from home just fine, and you put in the hours. Way too many hours. It's just, these things tell me you're getting sicker."

I nod, head low. This is my worst nightmare. Thought I was doing a better job of hiding all this.

"Can you tell me what's up? What's your doc saying?"

Take a breath, but not too big. Huff it out. *Think.*

"I dunno what's up," I say, "I've been to the GP in the past few months. He's run a few tests, but he doesn't seem to have much clue. Useless, just like the rest of 'em." I force a smirk and open my hands. "But it's okay, this'll pass eventually."

The furrowed lines on Alan's forehead are telling me he isn't buying my story. "Can't the GP send you to a specialist or something?"

"No," I lie. "That's not really an option."

I hate lying, and especially to my boss, but I hope he believed me. I've got no other choice. My future's looking the goods here and nothing and no-one's going to get in the way of that. Not even this health thing, whatever it damn well is.

··········

The knocking sound on my front door is unexpected. Very few people come to my place, so it sounds like a SWAT team pounding on my door with a battering-ram.

Things have been easier since I moved to this apartment on the west side of Karratha. I was in a company share house before and there were anything up to four people in the place. Hiding and managing my coughing fits and arse explosions had become impossible. I had to get out of there. And besides, I prefer being on my own.

As I reach for the door knob, the knocking sound comes again, and loud.

A waft of garlic, cooked salami, and melted cheese hits my nostrils as I open the door.

"Your pizza, Mr Malloy." It's Allie. She holds up a big pizza box with a flourish.

"Um, I didn't order a pizza."

"Yes you did." She pulls open the fly-screen door and pushes past me.

"Are Romeo's Pizza doing home invasions now?"

She calls back down the hallway, "All part of the service."

She should have smiled as she said that line, or even grinned a little. The joke would work better if she did. But I've still never seen Allie smile. She can hold her concrete block impression better than any stand-up comedian I've ever seen.

I follow her to the kitchen. *My* kitchen. It's like she knows her way around the place, even though she's never been here before.

"How did you know where I live?"

"Don't ask."

"I just did."

She ignores me and flips open the pizza box. Steam rises. More delicious aromas drift my way. "Where're your plates?" she asks as she proceeds to swing open every cupboard door within reach.

A few minutes later we're in the living room eating pizza, drinking beer, and watching TV like we've done this a hundred times before.

"What an *arse-wipe*," she says as she shakes her head at a politician on a TV news story, then eases out of her chair and grabs another slice of pizza.

Jeez, this girl can eat. How's she keep such a fit bod?

"Hah," is all I can manage in response as I pretend I'm *not* checking her out.

"Do ya like the pizza?" she asks. "I made sure it wasn't too spicy."

"Yeah, it's good. Thanks."

"Don't be awkward, dude," she says, her eyes still on the TV. "It's just *me*, you know."

I try to make a clever laughing sound and end up wheezing like a deflating balloon. So, I try to recover. "No, no. I mean, it's all good. It's cool."

"You weren't expecting company, I suppose," she says.

Talk about an understatement.

"Ah, well..."

Allie and I have connected a bit in the past few months, ever since the fan incident with Greg in the office. We say a few words at work here and there. A quick 'hey' and a nod when we pass each other. We've had a few chats in the tea room. The odd message and joke on the office chat app. We've eaten lunch together a few times.

But this—this change—this has floored me.

What's she doing here?

"There's nothing else for two loners to do on a Friday night in Karratha," she says with an overdone shrug.

"Yeah, good point."

She thinks I'm a loner?

Her eyes stay on the TV. "So, what's up with you being such a loner?"

I shrug, feeling self-conscious. "Dunno. It's just the way my cookie's crumbled."

"Right. So you're a fatalist as well, then."

Huh?

"Sorry, I haven't got a clue what that is."

"It wasn't a question," she says, flat as a board.

"Oh."

There's just silence now, apart from the TV news, so I grab another slice of pizza and take a bite.

What do I say next? Like, what do I do now?

The silence continues. I slip my phone out of my pocket.

She huffs. "You're googling the word *fatalist*, aren't you?"

"Yeah."

And Allie smiles for the first time.

13

Five months have passed, and she's actually smiling again, but on a screen this time. Well, it could be a smirk. That's Allie. She and I hang out a bit and I guess we've become friends. Not that I've got much choice in the matter.

"How's things there, dude?" she asks.

We chat through the usual stuff on the video call. I tell her what's happening in the office, and she tells me how she's going out on the Goodwyn platform.

She's actually pretty funny, in a dry sort of way. Her stories about working on oil and gas rigs in the middle of the ocean can be hilarious. The blokes out there wouldn't know what to make of her, I reckon.

"... and that's when I told him where he could stick his exploratory drill bit," she says, finishing her latest story.

The problem with laughing is it's not much different to coughing. The muscles, the nerves, how the air moves—it's the same. Which is why, as I'm laughing my head off now, my chest goes into another convulsion.

I drop my phone, stagger to the kitchen bench, and reef a heap of tissues out of the box. But then it *really* starts. The unstoppable coughing. The hacking. The irresistible urge to take in air and heave. The muscle contractions in my abdomen that squeeze all the messed-up mucus gobs out of my lungs and into my throat.

Another stagger now, to the place where I spend half my life: the toilet, to finish the purge.

It's five minutes before I make it back to the living room. Allie's face is still on my phone screen, with lines of worry now creasing her forehead.

"What's going on? Are you okay?"

"Don't worry. It just happens sometimes."

"I've noticed."

Bloody women and their intuition and their inbuilt radars. Thought I was doing a top job of keeping things under control and hidden. But, yeah … maybe not.

I cross my arms. "Can we change the subject?"

Allie huffs and puffs. "Okay. So how's things over at my place?"

"All good."

"How's Midnight?"

Her cat is black, shiny, and sleek. I don't like cats, but Midnight sure seems to like me. "Yeah, he's fine," I report. "He eats like a horse. And he won't leave me alone when I'm there."

She goes all gooey. "Aw, my boy is lonely. He must like you."

"I doubt it. But he won't bloody stop licking me. Does he do that to you?" I ask.

"Ah, no. No."

"Always licking my skin, he is. Weirdo."

She laughs. "Weird, yeah. It's funny, my little sister's cat used to—"

The sound stops. She looks frozen now on the screen.

"Allie?"

But nothing.

"Allie. Can you hear me?"

Finally, she shakes her head. Her eyes are like saucers now. "Yeah. Sorry…"

14

They're sitting on opposite sides of his desk. Staring hard. Staring right at each other.

I'm, like, a spectator or something.

It's the unmovable force: Doctor Wickramasinghe, versus the unstoppable force: Allie.

And then he breaks their staring match and gets up from his chair.

••••••••••

The loud knock on my door came earlier this morning, two days after the video call with Allie. I opened the door and there she was.

"Come with me," she said.

"What, no pizza this time?"

"Just get in the car."

I don't know why, but I just did as I was told.

We were in the doctor's surgery ten minutes later.

"But you don't have an appointment," the receptionist protested. "You can't—"

"We'll wait until he's free," Allie said. "This is important."

••••••••••

As the doctor gets out of his chair, I'm thinking it's all over. He'll do his usual, open the door and usher us out with a polite, "Good day, and see the receptionist on your way out."

I was surprised we even got in here. We'd waited ninety minutes before the receptionist got the idea we weren't going anywhere. She'd shown me into the consulting room with a scowl across her face. Allie had followed me in like she was meant to be there.

She didn't waste any time either. Started in on him even before she sat down. The poor doc couldn't deal with what hit him. He had no time to protest with any notions of privacy or permission—he was too busy answering Allie's rapid-fire questions.

After what seemed like ages, with them arguing about my tests and treatment, it had come down to a question of genetics, apparently.

Allie leaned forward. "He needs that genetic workup."

"Who says? Are you a doctor?" he asked, sharp as a scalpel.

She ignored him and ploughed on, leaning so far forward she was almost scooting across his desk. "You know as well as I do the test could rule in and out any number of things. You know this is right. And it's not like we're making a request for anything out of the ordinary, are we?"

We?

The doctor squinted hard and glared back at her. It was like he and Allie knew something, but were keeping me in the dark.

And now, as he crosses the room, he doesn't go for the door like I expected. He goes over to a cupboard and gets medical bits-n-pieces out and assembles them on a side counter. "Mr Malloy," he says, sounding all clinical and defeated at the same time, "please roll up your sleeve."

And I do.

••••••••••

"What was that all about?" I ask, as we get back to Allie's car.

"I'm just making sure he's covering all the bases," she says.

Why do I get the feeling she already has a certain base in mind?

I settle into the seat, still amazed she managed to do what I couldn't. "You sure as hell went hard at the guy. Have you had medical training, or something?"

"Me?" she sniggers, as we pull out of the car park. "Nah, I'm just an engineer."

Right.

••••••••••

It's three weeks later when I get the call from Doctor Wickramasinghe.

"Mr Malloy, we have your preliminary test results."

I close the boot of my car while holding the phone between my shoulder and head. The morning sun is trying to fry me in this supermarket car park—even at 8 AM. "Oh, okay. The genetic stuff?"

"Yes. It seems your girlfriend was right to insist on this test."

"Right, but she's not my girlfriend."

Hmm.

I drop my phone into a free hand. "What do the results say?

"There are some indicators of interest, but nothing conclusive at this point-in-time. You need further examination by a specialist to take this further."

Oh god, here we go again.

"I'm referring you to a specialist in Perth," he continues. "I have made the arrangements and she will see you next Friday. My receptionist will send you the details."

"Next Friday? What the? I can't—"

"Listen to me." His tone goes even flatter, as if that were possible. "This specialist is in very high demand and it is a minimum three-month wait to see her. She has made a special allowance for you at my request. Do *not* miss this opportunity."

Special allowance? It doesn't sound … good.

I get into my car, sweating beads, desperate to escape the sun and feel the air-con. "What's the rush, doc? Like, what's the deal? Can't you just fix this here?"

"She will explain everything. Make certain you are there next Friday. Good day."

The line goes dead. I reckon he failed phone consultations, too.

15

God, how I hate these places. Here I am, a week later, sitting in yet another medical consulting room, and in a hospital this time, in Perth. Strange, too, because the nurse told me I have to stay in this room and I can't have contact with the other patients.

Weird.

It took me two days to drive down here and I'm super-tired. Got little sleep overnight, and I had to stop every few hours to do the purges—from both ends.

No mucking around when I got here, either. Had to do a sweat test first up, which was odd, then lung function tests. If I'd had to blow in that gizmo and keep the little ball airborne one more time, I'm sure I would have passed out.

The doc asked me a bunch of questions to start with, and now she's reading reports and staying quiet. So I stare out her window and wonder what a gastroenterologist even does.

She looks up from her papers and adjust her glasses. "Dylan, your genetic tests came back with a few anomalies."

I'm outwardly cool, but inwardly going nuts. "Right."

"You have what's called a genetic mutation. It's called G-five-five-one. And we think there's likely another mutation we haven't identified yet."

So, I'm a mutant, or something?

I nod, like this means something to me. "Right."

"I'm sorry to say, your test results from today, and the gene mutation, are all pointing to a diagnosis of cystic fibrosis."

Huh? No asthma?

I scratch an arm. "Cystic what?"

"Cystic *Fibrosis*. We call it CF for short," she says, matter of fact.

I shake my head and shrug my shoulders. Not interested in anything new. "Never heard of it."

The doctor takes off her glasses, folds the arms, and sets them down on the desk. Then she inhales like she is about to deliver an epic story. Over the next fifteen minutes I learn what this CF thing is. One in four people carry the gene which causes CF and most don't even realise. I learn how my parents' genes were the wrong combination. I learn how mutated genes cause proteins in my body to act weird. My cells can't use salt to attract water to their surface like normal people, which means the mucus in my organs gets thick and sticky and doesn't clear from my body like it should.

At first, I was feeling all defensive and thinking this just can't be. But it all starts making sense as she explains the symptoms and what happens. The mucus, yeah, I know *all about* the mucus. Here I was thinking yellow and green were normal. And the problems with my gut. The stomach aches. Salty sweat and salty taste. The fatigue. All that.

I ask her a few questions. I need to know what this thing means for my work and maybe where I live. Then I go for the jugular, for the sixty-four million dollar question: "So, what's the cure?"

She pauses and swallows. "I'm afraid we don't have a cure. Not yet, anyway. Our treatments are improving, but progress is slower than we'd like. CF doesn't always get the government support or funding some other diseases do."

"So..." I feel frozen in my chair, trying to get my head around what she's saying. "Are you saying I'll have this thing for the rest of my life?"

She holds her gaze steady at me. "Based on what we currently know, yes. This is a lifelong condition."

Those words hit me hard for a second, but I somehow keep the cool act going. "Right. I guess I'll just have to try to manage it, then. I can't let this get in the way of my work."

"Yes, there are ways you can manage CF. And we're here to help you with those. Our clinic will support you all the way."

All the way?

"Okay, great, but, it's like ... like, you're not telling me something?"

"This is difficult to say, and will be difficult for you to hear, Dylan." She pauses and does her best to hide a visible gulp. "But you need to understand. The average lifespan for a CF patient in Australia is about forty years. Some patients live longer than forty, but others do not make it past childhood or even their twenties."

I'm not sure what she says next. The room is spinning. Her words seem jumbled and *forty* keeps bouncing off other erratic thoughts racing in and out of my head. Crazy, stupid thoughts. Some relevant, some not.

I hear her voice, like it's down a tunnel. "Dylan?"

"Ah, yep."

"I realise this must be a big shock for you, it always is for CF patients, and there is much to take in. But there is some good news."

I slump back in my chair. "For real? I could sure do with some right now."

She explains how my unique mutations meant CF went undetected as a kid. It's called a late diagnosis CF. A fancy way of saying my CF is rare. The symptoms showing up in my early teens looked like other things—like asthma and bronchitis—and had the doctors fooled. People with late diagnosis CF are often not diagnosed until their twenties or even later.

Guess I'm one of them.

"... and the good news," she says, "is you don't have all the chronic conditions which many CF sufferers get. We've got more tests to conduct, but we think your liver and kidneys are not significantly affected at this stage."

At this stage? There are stages?

"Right."

She shuffles some papers. "Now. We'll be booking you in for a series of appointments over the next week, and—"

"The next week? No. No way." I shake my head emphatically. Everything inside me is screaming: bolt from this office and run. "I have to drive back tomorrow. I've got work to do. People are relying on me back there, you know."

She slips her glasses on and sits up. "Whatever else you have in your diary, you must cancel it. This is too important."

"But—"

A hand goes up, as does her volume. "*Dylan*, your life depends on this."

···········

I'm sitting in my car trying to process what just happened.

I'm kinda scared, but relieved, too. At least I understand what this thing is now, and why my body does what it does. But I'm not sure if the relief of knowing is much better than the fear of not knowing. Did I win the lottery, or did I get a death sentence?

And the doctor—this Professor Hardy lady—seems to know what she's doing, unlike all those other doctors in the past. Her card says she's a respiratory physician, not a gastroenterologist.

And my mind keeps wandering and my brain calculates ahead. I can't say I've ever had my life planned out—far from it. But, no matter what my life's going to be like, I thought I had, like, eighty or ninety years to do everything. But I've only got another fifteen years if I'm lucky. So, what should I do? Hit the fast-forward button? I mean, how much can I pack-in before I … pack it in?

And then there's my work and career.

My phone buzzes with a message. No surprise who it is…

Allie: Hey. What'd they say?

Me: Not now. I'll talk to you when I get back

Allie: OK. C U Sunday

Me: No can do. I'll be here for another week

Allie: A week. What's going on?

Me: Not now. Later

··········

The next week became a blur.

More tests. More results. More chats with Professor Hardy and the other doctors.

Then came the medications. Nurses and therapists training me to use gadgets to help clear my lungs. Physios teaching me exercises and cuckoo breathing techniques. And this dietitian woman telling me what to eat and what not to eat. I got more education than I learned in the whole of high school, and that's no joke.

Then referrals to a physio in Karratha.

And then goodbye, for now.

As I drive out the hospital car park on the final day, I'm glad to be getting away from here. They've been super-great, all those clinic people, but I need space and time. It hasn't all sunk in yet and my head feels like it'll burst.

I turn onto the Mitchell Freeway to head north and this thought drops into my head. A memory. Unwanted and awkward. I try to get rid of it, but the thing just won't budge.

I hang a left and exit the freeway. There's something here I need to make right.

••••••••••

The garden's not its usual spectacular self. The lawn is sparse and brown, and the beds are overgrown and missing their spring colour. I stop at the familiar old front door, clench and unclench my fists, and take a big breath. It's been two-and-a-half years since I last crossed this threshold.

Knock, knock.

Knock, knock, knock.

Long seconds pass. Birds tweet. Insects buzz.

I knock again.

There's more long seconds before the door opens a few centimetres and a short moon-faced lady is staring up at me through the gap. I've never seen her before. She's got a grumbling, dribbling baby hooked on her hip.

"Oh, hi. Is Nancy here?" I ask, trying not to appear surprised.

"Nancy? No Nancy," she snaps, and goes to close the door.

What the hell?

I put a hand out to keep the door open. "Nancy Medhurst. She owns this place."

"*No*. Husband buy house last year," she says in a thick accent. "House empty, then."

I don't understand. I start to ask, "Do you have her new—"

Her whining kid begins to scream.

"You go now," the woman says as she flicks a hand at me.

She pushes the door shut with a thud, and I hear the door lock behind me as I turn for the front path. The solid clunk all but says: *don't you ever come back*.

I can't even look at the place as I take my final walk down that front path. My eyes are on anything but the house as I retreat to the car and drive off. Yet another person's gone, it seems. Most likely forever. Another significant someone out of my life.

But as I push down the accelerator and the white lines of the Mitchell Freeway come at me faster and faster ... *flick* ... *flick* ... *flick* ... the guy's voice comes back to me. His words are so clear and his tone so insistent, it's like the old fella's right here.

'So, don't go and do what I did, Dylan. No matter how shitty some other people can be, when you come across people you can trust—stick with 'em. That's all I can say.'

And it dawns on me as I think through what just happened, and how things ended up with Nancy a few years back. For the first time: it wasn't about someone else jumping ship on me. Nope, it had been *me* who'd left. And with hardly a goodbye.

16

"Yes," Allie says.

I search her eyes. "Did you hear what I said?"

"Yes. I get it."

I'm not sure what I was expecting from Allie as I explained CF and my prognosis to her on my return to Karratha, but sympathy or understanding didn't seem to be happening. I don't know what I need or want right now, but a cool logical engineer's response is not doing it for me. Not at all.

"I guess, I—"

Allie turns away and faces the kitchen window. Her eyes are closed and her mouth held tight.

What's with her?

"You okay?" I ask.

She nods, but her eyes and mouth don't budge.

So I continue, "What I don't understand is how you seemed to know, like, after that video call you were on a mission about this. What gives?"

She turns slowly and faces me. "It was the cat."

The cat? I don't care about the frickin cat.

"Remember how Midnight was licking your skin?" she says. "Cats do it because they like the taste of the salt."

"Ah, right. But how did you connect the dots? You're not a doctor, just an engineer, like you said."

"Doesn't matter." She gives a tight shrug and I don't have to be a body language expert to see she doesn't want to tell me.

I thrust up both my hands and half yell, without thinking, "*It matters to me.*"

Allie puffs out a breath and looks down at her fingers. She's furiously rubbing at a split in a fingernail. "My sister's cat used to do the same thing. To her."

"It licked her skin, you mean?"

"Yeah."

"How come?"

She looks up at me with those dark eyes, all glassy and wide now.

And the thought clicks in my head—a revelation—and my guts grip and turn. "Your sister … she has CF?"

She nods and looks down again. "Diagnosed at birth."

I step back, grab the bench top behind me, and whisper, "Oh my god."

"I gotta go." She grabs her keys and spins around on the chair as if she'd just been told to evacuate.

"Wait. Look. I'm sorry," I say as I follow her down the passage. "Ah, how is your sister handling it? Is she okay?"

Allie stops halfway across the front patio, but doesn't turn. "She's gone," she says in a whisper. "We lost her six years ago."

••••••••••••

Allie was back a half-hour later, her eyes red, her face still pale.

Those thirty minutes without her were more like hours. For once, time alone wasn't what I'd needed. All the possibilities swam and screamed in my head like a vicious whirlpool pulling me down. Treatment, and drugs, and routines, and physio are all something, but they just sank to the bottom of my mind. Alarming thoughts clamoured near the surface and blotted-out all the others.

What are my chances? Will I also die young?

"I'm sorry," she says, eyes down on her feet. "Sorry about that. It's all still pretty raw. Even more than I thought."

"It's okay, Allie. I get it." I try to usher her inside but she doesn't move. Just looks up and our eyes lock for a few seconds.

"This isn't about my sister though," she says, "or me. Not anymore. We need to focus on *you*."

"We?" I ask.

"Who else, dickhead?"

"But, why me?"

"I think all CF people ask that question at some point or another."

"No, no, I mean, why do *you* want to help *me*?"

Allie screws up her face and folds her arms. "We're mates. Enough said."

"But—"

Her hands grab her hips now. "Fark's-sake, Dylan. You think too much. Don't look for reasons all the time, just … you know … *be*."

"Right."

17

Just be?

Hmm.

Six months later, I'm struggling with what my life has become. The endless daily routines of treatment. I have to clear my lungs at night and again in the morning using these insane gadgets. The blowing and wheezing and hacking. Steroid medications and supercharged antibiotics to stop bugs from living in my mucus and scar tissue. Ever-increasing amounts of enzyme pills to help with digestion every time I eat, and daily handfuls of vitamins. Shake me and I will rattle. And the diet is pretty strict. I'm trying to keep weight on, but it's a struggle no matter how much stuff I swallow.

Not everything's bad, though. The routines seem to be making a difference. My bowel issues are more manageable, and I feel like my energy level is up a bit. The lung events are better during the day, although it's worse at night sometimes. But if I'm consistent with all this, and if I do all the little things, I might be okay.

Allie is on her feet, bouncing and stretching like some over-enthusiastic recruit at an army camp. "*C'mon.* The rain'll be here soon. Time to get out there."

She's like this cross between Nurse Betty and a personal trainer from the pit of hell. A task master who won't take *no* for an answer.

We're in the wet season when the air outside is stickier than glue and people around here go nuts with the heat. But not her, unfortunately. She understands the need for routine better than me I guess, so I shut up and do what I'm told—most of the time.

"Yeah, yeah. Whatever," I say, as I shove on my sports shoes.

"I'm gonna tell, otherwise."

"I don't remember giving you Professor Hardy's number."

"You didn't. Your phone did."

"Oh, so you two are on talking terms now, or what?"

"It's girl business. Stay out of it."

"But—"

Her bouncing stops and her hands go on hips. "You wanna end up back at the medical centre again? An hour working out with me has got to be better than more days lying flat on your back hooked up to drips."

Allie knows full well I hate being admitted to hospital when the infections go nuts, and each visit to the place is like a mini-defeat.

Yeah, nah. There's no way outta this.

So I just mumble to myself as I fiddle with my shoelaces and dread the hour of torture ahead.

••••••••••

My mobile buzzes two days later.

Better take this one.

"Dylan. It's Professor Hardy here. Got a minute?"

"Sure." I head out of the office to keep the call private.

"We received your latest scans from the hospital in Port Headland, and we've been analysing the data from your CF app."

"Right."

I want this news to be good, but I know it won't be. Her news rarely is.

"We're concerned about the scar tissue in your lungs. It's increasing, I'm afraid. So I've booked you in for some further scans and treatment here at the end of this month. My secretary will email you the details."

"Wow. Okay. Guess I'll have to drive down. Again."

Bugger it.

....

A week later, I'm not sure if the scenery looks any better from a car or a bus. It's the same flat nothingness of red orange dirt. The same boring bone-dry shrubs. The same never-ending faded black highway to Perth.

"Did you get the email?" Allie said to me as we chomped on takeaway noodles at her place a week earlier.

"What email?"

"The one from Professor Hardy's office." She kept her gaze firmly on her noodle box.

"Yes, I got that one. Just like you, it seems. Whatever happened to patient privacy?"

She turned a fraction and winked at me. "It's cool. We've got a special arrangement."

"Oh wow, is that right?"

Minutes later, Allie was busy clicking away on her laptop.

"You searching for engineer porn again?"

She gave me a thumbs-down. "*Ba-bow* ... just looking-up some flights."

"Hmm. Are you going somewhere?"

"Flights for *you*, dickhead. For Perth, next week."

I got to my feet as my mind scrambled. "For me? Perth? What the hell?"

A big shake of her head, then she lifted her eyes to the ceiling. "You can't drive there and back again, not the way things are. You know that."

"Yeah, but I don't fly."

Ugh, why the hell did I say that? Those bloody words—my words—knifed me before they'd finished spilling from my mouth. It drives me nuts: no matter how many years have passed or how far across the country I've come, that bit of my past is still *there*.

Allie gave me yet another head shake, her face all screwed up. "What is it with you and flying?" she insisted. "Are you a pussy or something?"

"Up yours," I said, deflating back to the couch.

"The goss around work is you're shit-scared of getting on a chopper." She studied my face, looking for something. "But it's the big planes too, huh? You won't fly in anything, is that your deal?"

"Mind your own business." I wasn't talking about this. I flicked on the TV to reinforce my need for privacy and distraction.

"Whatever you say." She snapped the laptop shut. "But that means I'll be driving."

And so, a week later, it's precisely what's happening as my car hums down the highway towards Perth, with Allie at the wheel.

....

A day later, we're finally getting close to the city and passing the outlying town of Pearce. I'm so sick and tired of Highway One. It's tedious not driving, and in my car to make it worse, but the slightly greener landscape and the appearance of signs of real civilisation are starting to give me a better vibe.

Allie's been rabbiting on about something or other for god knows how long. She's funny like that: a bit crap at talking in unfamiliar social situations, but happily entertains herself for ages by talking to herself when I'm around. If I'm too zoned-out or bored to listen, I'll drop in a 'yeah', or a 'right', or a 'hah' every now and again when it seems right, which keeps her talking on unawares. She'll keep going then. On and on, and on…

"… and dad didn't flinch when Barry told him about it. Like, he just sat there with this big smile on his face and pretended—"

A shadow flicks over the car, blotting out the sun for a microsecond, and then we're hit with this extreme *whoosh* and a sonic *boom*, like something's exploded overhead. Car windows rattle. Time freezes. Allie actually shuts up. I grope for the dash to hang on to something. Anything.

Allie yells above the subsiding boom, "What the?" as the car veers into the middle of the road before she wrestles it back to the left-hand lane.

It's then I see it as I squint at the sky, and I point up and beyond the windscreen.

She cranes her head forward above the steering wheel and her mouth drops open when she spots the object—a small, fast-moving jet streaking away from us at an insanely low altitude.

"Prick," I say, shaking my head knowingly. "Must be doing low-level ops and thought he'd have some fun."

"Huh?" Allie grunts, her head and face still contorted and staring at the thing. "Is that, like an F-18, or what?"

"Nah. Hawk 127 out of Pearce RAAF base," I say, "from 79 Squadron, and on a nap-of-the-earth training sortie, no doubt."

I'm smiling to myself as I watch the jet disappear over a small hill, self-satisfied with the aviation wiki which somehow still lives secretly inside my head, when I realise I've just said those words out loud.

Damn. Now I'll have to divert her.

Too late. Allie's face has gone blank and hard like she's heard a ghost. The car's indicator is blinking and we're pulling off the road into a rest area.

As the car comes to a stop, she cuts the ignition, yanks on the handbrake, folds her arms, and turns to me. "*What. The. Hell.*"

"It's okay," I try, waving my hand at the windscreen distractedly. "We can go. It's gone now and no harm's done. Are you alright?"

"Me?" she scoffs. "It's not *me* we need to talk about, is it?"

I shrug.

"How the hell do you know about all that?" she begins, waving a hand in circles in the air. "How can someone who hates flying to the point they'll poo their jocks at even the thought of getting on a damn plane, know so much about them? It just does *not* add up."

She's right: it's never added up. But that's my business.

I shrug again. "Dunno."

"Pure flummery. I've seen how you always look up when a plane goes past."

I turn and stare back down the highway. I don't know why. It's as if something's coming. Something's giving chase and getting closer by the minute.

Allie huffs, checks the rear-vision mirror, then looks out the front windscreen. She unfolds her tight-locked arms and says, "Dylan, look. I think it's time you levelled with me on this. You and I, we know each other pretty good. You get me probably better than anyone else, I know. And I think I got you sussed, mostly. But there's some things you're not telling me. Important things. I just know it."

This is like I'm back in the old guy's truck now, stuck there as a passenger with nowhere to go. Stuck there hearing questions I don't want to answer. Stuck there facing things I want to forget.

"I want to know," she continues. "I think I *need* to know, what's really going on with you. What is it with you and this weirdness about flying?"

There's the *tick … tick … tick* sound of the engine cooling. The distant whine of wheels on bitumen. The sharp pant of my breath. The rest of it, everything else here, has gone dark. Like I'm in a cocoon or something, as if I'm no longer really here.

"Dylan, Dylan," I hear Allie's voice calling to me, her words echoing and fading.

"Dylan, Dylan." The words come again, but this time, the voice is not hers...

·····•·····

Eight years earlier, Melbourne

"… Dylan, Dylan."

"Huh?" I mumble.

"*Dylan.*"

Someone's shaking me. I get an eye open. Early morning. I focus on the clock-radio: *6:58a.m.* "What?"

"I need to talk to you," her voice says.

"Not now. I'll be up later," I say, turning over with a huff.

Aunt Cheryl's voice sounds hushed and shaky. "Dylan, we need to talk. It's important."

So much for a sleep-in.

She sits on the bed near my feet. Her eyes are like hubcaps and she's white as powder. "I have to tell you something."

I rub my eyes and half sit-up. "Yeah, what?"

"It's … it's your mum," she says in a whisper.

"Mum?" I yawn. "Okay, what's up?"

Aunt Cheryl goes to say more words but her mouth like hangs open. Her lower jaw is trembling. There's this teardrop escaping her left eye and starting down her cheek.

Something knifes through my guts. *What the hell is going on here?* "Shit. What? What's wrong?" I demand.

"I'm sorry. Her plane. Her flight … on the way back, she…"

No.

I snatch my phone off the bedside table, flick-on the tracker app, and quickly locate flight KX72. The flight status says: *DELAYED.* As the map view zooms in on eastern Europe, the *KX72* aircraft symbol is mid-air in the middle of nowhere and not moving.

"What the hell's going on?" I yell at Aunt Cheryl.

But she's full-on sobbing now, head in her hands, no more words are coming.

Without thinking, I flick my phone over to a national news site and hit the *Latest stories* link.

And my entire world comes crashing down.

O2

Present day, Western Australia

"My god," Allie says, barely audible. "I'm sorry. I just. I just never knew."

I wipe the damp from my face with a hand, then my sleeve, turning to face the paddocks out the passenger-side window. But there's no relief, not even out there. No comfort. No escape. For there, out on the endless rolling fields of unharvested wheat, I see them. Pieces of fuselage. Torn, jagged pieces of metal, falling. The spinning entrails of a dying jet engine thumping into the soil. Pieces of cabin lining drifting down like leaves. Showers of tiny debris that fall like snow and rain, yet burn. And seats—still joined in rows of two, three—twisting, tumbling, then hammering, unbelievably, to the earth. And passengers, humans … people.

I don't know how long we sat there. No idea if Allie said anything further. Or me. No clue when she started the car and got us back on the road. But an hour later, my head has somehow come back to the present and I realise we've stopped again and in a car park, somewhere in Perth.

"You okay?" she asks.

I nod.

She looks contemplative. "Things make more sense now. About flying, why you never mention your mum, all those things."

"Yeah."

"I'm sorry it all came up like it did, I didn't mean to—"

"Hey, don't stress," I say, not wanting her to feel bad. She's had enough loss in her own life. "Like you said, it was time I levelled with you. And I don't think I've really ever dealt with it anyway … for myself, I mean."

"I can only imagine," she says in a hush. "And how old were you? Must have been so hard to deal."

"Fifteen. And yeah, it was the worst. Still is. I still think about what I could've done … should've done."

Allie looks at me like I'm crazy. "Dude, you were fifteen, and the plane was half a world away."

I hold my eyes shut as tight as they'll go and speak the words out loud I've never said, "Yeah, but I had this feeling. And I knew the airline and its history. And I knew the route they'd be taking. And I just knew I shoulda said something. I shoulda told her that last time I spoke to her on the phone. I should've told her to cancel and get another flight. But I was too damn selfish. I just wanted her back. I *needed* her home. So I kept my stupid mouth shut and hoped for the best."

"You blame yourself? You've been doing that this whole time?" she asks.

I shrug hard and open my eyes. "Guess so. But I think I want to drop this subject for now, okay?"

Allie nods. "Yeah, yeah, of course, But, do you mind if ask you one more thing?" she says, sheepish.

I take another deep breath. "Okay."

"Like, I get why you're totally off flying—that's understandable—but before the accident happened, was flying your thing?"

"Yep. It was."

"Your dream?"

It all comes flooding back. My plans. Everything I'd learned. The career I'd wanted. "Yeah. I was going to be a pilot. I had it all mapped out."

The thought hits me: I've not said anything like those words in over eight years.

"And that's why you're so head-strong about your work now, and being an IT hot shot? It's all a stand-in for what you really wanted to do, and be?"

As Allie's question hangs in the air, I can hear the old guy's voice again:

"*... there's also running from something. We can deny, switch, and avoid our past all we like. But one day, the thing you run from is gonna come get ya.*"

I have no more words for Allie now. All I can do is nod.

She puts a hand on mine and stares down at them, clasped together tight on the edge of my seat. Her face is drawn but soft, strained but also peaceful. It's a look of understanding. Of compassion. Of much more than words could ever say.

Allie's face and her calm presence tell me I'm *here*. I'm right here in the present, in the here-and-now. And somehow, no matter what's behind me, *here* might be okay.

18

Am I attending a local book club? Have I been magically transported into a beauty salon?

Here I was thinking this was a doctor's office.

Allie and Professor Hardy seem right in their element, though, regardless of the setting. "Oh, hey, it's *so* good to meet you in person..."; "thanks so much for your texts..."; "how's it going with..."; "oh, I know, I know..."; and laughter, and grins, and enough hand gestures to create mid-air turbulence.

But a few minutes in, I have to interrupt their impenetrable chat. "Hi," I say loudly, "my name's Dylan, and I'm a CF-er."

Allie presses her lips together and sighs.

Professor Hardy stops and blinks, then smiles. "Sorry, Dylan. It's just, Allie and I have been communicating quite a bit, but we hadn't actually met yet. It's nice to finally catch-up, you know, face-to-face."

"Yeah, I can see that," I say. "Allie's told me all about your secret girl business."

"It's rather unconventional, yes." The professor is actually blushing. "But it *is* necessary. An unconventional approach to manage a very unconventional challenge."

I scratch my head. "I've been called lots of things, but never that."

"It's how you deal with things around CF, Dylan. You want to know what's happening, but your standard reaction seems to be to avoid the full truth and just plod on with what you can handle. Unfortunately, ignoring something doesn't stop it existing. We need to get you past that."

Allie shifts in her seat and coughs.

This is sounding … heavy. I sit forward. "And that's why you've brought me here? To tell me more bad news?"

Professor Hardy's smile has evaporated to her usual clinical look. "No. I've already outlined how we're concerned with your lungs and how they're going. We need to run another series of tests and see where things are at. That's why we've brought you down here. Once we've got the results, I might actually have some better news for you."

"Not more frickin tests?"

"Yes," the professor sighs. "More frickin tests. Now…"

••••••••••

I'd expected a few hours of the usual breathe into a gizmo, make the ball hover, blow till you nearly pass out tests. Been there and done them so many times.

But today was different. I had a whole team of people working on me. Not just one psychologist, but two. They each interviewed me separately, then together. Mountains of questions about my work, lifestyle, diet, relationships. And I started thinking, *what's all this about? Where is this going?*

Then they took more blood than a vampire. "Just for some more tests," the nurse said as she extracted the third vial of red stuff.

And another nurse did the opposite. There were more and more needles, but he was putting stuff into me this time. Apparently I'm now vaccinated against every nasty bug ever discovered.

More talks with other doctors; each with their own checklists. Other scans, x-rays and stuff. Then a dentist. Yep, a dental check-up was the icing on this weird-as cake.

I didn't see Allie again until late afternoon in Professor Hardy's waiting room.

"Hey dude. How are you coping?" Allie asks as I sit beside her.

"If they put another hole in me, I reckon I'll shrivel up. And I'm all talked out, I just want to get out of here."

She puts a hand loosely on top of mine. "Hang in there, it's all good."

I've had a whole day of gloved medical hands touching me, but Allie's touch is skin-to-skin, and warm.

She waves circles with her other hand. "This is just what you gotta do, and you're nearly all done now. I'm sure Jane will put your mind at ease."

"Jane?"

"Yeah, Jane. You know, Professor Hardy."

"Right."

••••••••••

I look at the doctor, then at Allie, then back at the doctor. "Someone else's lungs inside my chest—inside *me*?"

"Yes," Professor Hardy, aka Jane, replies flatly. "That's how the lung transplant process works."

"But why? How? I mean, why on earth would we need to do something so crazy as that?"

"It's why I asked you to come to Perth and go through those tests, Dylan. The deterioration of your lungs is not at the stage where you need a transplant right now, but experience tells us we need to be ahead of the game and be sure you are eligible for a transplant when it becomes necessary."

"Why didn't you tell me what this was about, like, last week or this morning?"

"Because I knew you'd never come down, or even do the tests. *Unconventional,* remember?"

Allie clears her throat.

"Wow." I look to the ceiling and hold in the urge to cough. The light fitting above my head seems to be slowly spinning.

This can't be happening.

"And does he … does he meet all the criteria?" I hear Allie's voice ask. She sounds like a child asking for something they shouldn't have.

"This is the good news. Yes. Dylan meets the criteria." The professor turns back to me. "We're putting you on the transplant list. There were some concerns about your willingness to comply and stick with the routines, but I went in to bat for you on those points. I assured the team that, with Allie around, you will stay on track."

This last week is making sense now. There's been a coordinated plan all along to get me here, although I think the whole transplant angle has taken even Allie by surprise. Her face is even more pale than usual.

"How long will I need to wait?" I ask, hardly recognising my own voice.

"For the transplant? Depends on your condition and how things go from here. Once we get to the point where you must have the transplant—when the benefits clearly outweigh the risks—it could be a matter of weeks, a few months, maybe up to a year. It all hangs on when a compatible donor becomes available."

Of course. It's not like they have lungs just lying around.

We asked more questions. She gave us more answers. The operation would take half a day and I'd be in hospital for three weeks. Then I'd be on new drugs and new treatments for the rest of my life.

"Buy why," I ask her, "like, why would I even bother with all of it? It's all nuts!"

Professor Hardy takes off her glasses and sets them neatly in front of her. She looks at Allie, then at me. "Because without donor lungs, Dylan, your prognosis is likely to become very poor, very quickly. Your life expectancy will drop considerably. We could be talking months."

Allie's voice is thin and shaky now. "And with donor lungs?"

"Once our patients get through the first year following a transplant, they will usually live a much healthier, happy life for another five to ten years, and even up to twenty years. Some even longer."

More numbers. More probability. More vague hope. But what does it all mean?

"And then?" Allie says.

"And then some patients will need another transplant. But as I've said, there are risks along the way and not every patient makes it through each procedure. I must be clear about this." She turns to me, her eyes glassy. "But it can buy you time, Dylan, and much better quality of life in the meantime. And our treatments are improving all the time."

I slump back and hold my head. The light fitting is spinning even faster now.

19

We make it back to the hotel in Perth as it's getting dark. Got no idea what the time is.

It was all too much to handle. Way too hectic. Too cray-cray, as Allie would say. She's five years older than me, but this transplant thing may be too much, even for her. We're too young for all this crap.

So we raid the bar fridge in Allie's room and sink shots, not giving a stuff about the scary price list on the wall. Allie throws a little green pill down her throat, washes it down with another shot, and hands me a yellow pill. It looks like a kid's lolly, complete with a smiley face embedded into the surface.

"What's this?" I ask.

"A pick-me-up for a night off from CF. You'll feel all gucci."

"Right. And why's this one yellow?"

"Shut up and swallow."

I'll pay for this. Big time. I'll get lit, yeah, but it'll take days to get back from the mother of all hangovers. But, whatever, just do what the engineer says.

••••••••••

The midnight hour has come and gone.

Allie sits on the bed, head in her hands, her fingers buried in her jet-black hair.

Fatigue, the booze, and some unsettling chemical reaction wash over and through me. I'm on the sofa with my head back staring at the ceiling and empty of words.

Boredom, or the comedown, or both, seem to kick in as Allie looks up. "Imagine having bits of someone else's body, like, become part of yours. How mental is that?"

"I don't even want to think about it."

"But isn't it awesome what they can do? You get new lungs and a new life."

"Not new lungs. *Used* lungs," I insist. "Some broken loser's ex-lungs."

"So? They were gonna cark-it, anyway."

"But they haven't gone topside yet, have they? Someone compatible with me is going to have to die so I can live. There's no guarantee it'll ever happen."

I try to imagine if, when, and how all of it could even be, but it's an impossible thing to comprehend.

"Yeah, but your blood type's very common, so we can only hope, huh?" she says, dry as a cracker.

"Tell that to their family."

Minutes tick past. Away in my thoughts. My imagination wanders through the haze of my future and the possibilities, with my brain still calculating things in years and months. The lung transplant has a fair chance of improving my quality of life and might give me extra years too, which'd be sweet, I guess. But the surgery and recovery are mega, and there's the risks.

Right now, though, duty is calling. The usual fluid and gunk are building deep in my chest and it won't be long before my expert swallow-and-hold routine will give way and I have to do the deed again.

"I better head back to my room and do my physio," I say. "I'll catch you in the morning."

Allie springs to her feet. "Wait."

And as I stand there at the door she moves closer, reaches out her hand, and lifts one of mine into hers. She keeps her gaze down as her thumb rubs back-and-forth across my fingers.

This feels different.

Things surge through and around. Time speeds up and goes slow-mo in the same moment. Emptiness grips in my guts. A building unease of not knowing what to say or do. And there's this zap of energy like an electric charge, or something. It holds me, like frozen solid, and I can't make my feet move.

She looks up at me, but her eyes don't quite meet mine. "You could … stay," she says, her voice thin and hushed.

"Allie. I, um, like, I wish…"

"Don't be shy," she says. "It's just *me,* you know."

My breath is almost gone now, but I somehow get the next words out. "It's, it's what happens with me … overnight. With my CF. It's really ugly and you can't see that."

She looks straight into my eyes. Her face is going blank like something's just pulled the plug out of her being and her life-force is draining, fast.

I drag my hand back from hers as gently as I can. "You understand CF more than most, but believe me, it's worse than even you can understand. Nobody knows what I go through at night, and nobody else should have to see it. And nobody should have to be kept awake because of my coughing fits. No one else but me."

"Dude, I can—"

"No." My head shakes and my eyes go the floor. "I can't do that to you."

••••••••••

The walk along the corridor to my hotel room is the worst thing ever. It's as if I'm a prisoner on death row and heading for the chamber. Or a con artist who duped his best friend. Or a misguided loser who told the most beautiful woman in the world he was leaving to join a monastery.

But, relationships? Or even a family one day? The thoughts make me shiver.

Some people spend their time planning their dream wedding. I find myself plotting out how my funeral will go.

And I get how the logic works, too. With families, and with kids, and all that. I've thought about it over and over in the empty night hours when the coughing won't let up. A partner shouldn't have to lose their other half when so much of their own life is still to come. And kids don't want a parent who checks out on them before their mid-teens. I know how it goes.

But even worse, two partners hooking-up when both of them have the CF gene in their families is asking for trouble. Rolling the one-in-four dice which determines whether a kid gets CF isn't a game I'm ever willing to play.

Nope.

As I assemble all the pills and the nebuliser and the other paraphernalia to do my physio, the possibility of a lung transplant seems a million miles off. I'm wondering how much more this invisible monster can steal from me. I think I know the final answer, but I deny it. Like I always do. Like I must.

20

We never mentioned the big deal, the 'incident' between us in the hotel room in Perth. It was too painful for me, and I think way too awkward for Allie. And she hasn't asked me anything further about the whole flying thing either, or about my mum. It all kinda sits there in a locked Pandora's box.

Which is fine, because there's been plenty to distract us since we got back to Karratha seven months ago. There's been lots happening at work and I've thrown myself into it all like there was no next year. Allie's been away on the rigs for weeks at a time, but she's managed my exercise program, my diet, and kept my head somewhere near sane, whether she's been onshore or off. She's trying super-hard, even by remote control from distant oil platforms. And I'm doing everything I can to hold on to whatever remaining health I have, and keep working.

But it's just not enough.

Two nasty bacterial infections have hit me in the past eight weeks. Frickin things. Spent a whole week in isolation in the local hospital on IV antibiotics. And my lung function is still declining and sometimes near thirty percent now, but I don't need a test to tell me that. It's as if I'm slowly drowning. Drowning within myself.

Like I'm fighting to stay afloat, straining for air. And with each breath I take, more time slips away.

I'd never say it, but I think this thing has got me. I'm not sure how much longer I can fight on.

Greg gets up from his desk and holds the door open as I leave the upstairs office at work. "G'day," he says, hushed and even.

"G'day," I reply.

"Thanks, mate," I say as I wheel my new accomplice behind me—the oxygen bottle that goes with me everywhere. I'm permanently strapped to this nasal tube with two prongs jammed-up my nostrils. Yes, this thing keeps me conscious, but jeez, it's like I'm carrying around a sign that says: 'HEY, I'M DEFEATED. DEAD SOON'.

A side benefit of the O_2 bottle, though, is it's also like a sign that says: 'YEP, I'M ACTUALLY PRETTY CROOK'. Until now, people who found out about my CF have reacted in strange ways. Some treat me like I've picked a convenient syndrome such as chronic fatigue, or something. A few people ask what CF is, but they go blank and their eyes glaze over as I try to explain it for the millionth time. Others say things like, 'but you don't look sick' or 'you seem pretty normal'. A few have said to me, 'you'll live well past forty years'. But how do they know? And one guy at work even said, 'Oh yeah, pulmonary fibrosis … my grandad had that.'

"You okay?" Greg asks.

I wheeze. "Yeah, I'm okay."

Gone are the days of silly nicknames and office antics. Gone is the schoolboy gossip. There's despair written on Greg's face, now. And pity, too, I think. Helplessness. He's like a man chained to a river bank watching another man drown, in slow motion.

He follows me into the foyer. “If there’s anything I can do, I want you to know I’m here for ya.” He jags a thumb back at office area, “We all are, mate. We got your back.” His eyes are wide and blinking fast.

I go to respond, but can only give him a strained smile and a raised hand as I cough and splutter and pant out some heavy breaths. Which is alright, in a weird sort of a way, because I don’t really have a clue what to say to him.

“Take care,” Greg says as I get to the stairs.

I wave, pick up my oxygen bottle, and start the slow journey to the ground floor. It’s still just one flight of stairs, but it feels more like ten these days. With each step, my mind runs through the people here; the many good people who give a toss. I know they appreciate me as a colleague, CF or not. I get it. They value the work I’ve done, and there’s so much more for me to do here, too. I just never thought my connections to these people would go any further.

It’s all a bit like CF, I guess: very hard to comprehend.

••••••••••

I’m gripping my phone so hard I reckon it might fall to bits and hit the ground in a hundred pieces. I kinda wish it would. But I close my eyes and keep speaking into the damn thing. “I don’t think I can do that,” I say.

But Professor Hardy isn’t backing off. “Dylan. Please hear me out. The climate up there is working against you. We think it’s making you more susceptible to infection. You can’t risk another run-in with one of those bugs.”

“But this is where I live and work. I’m needed here.”

"*Priorities*, Dylan. Keeping you alive and healthy is number one and nothing else should matter. You need to be in Perth where we can provide the therapy you need and keep you on the list. And you need to be here ... if it happens."

"If what happens?"

"If you get a donor."

The thought of someone else's lungs still rattles me to the core. "Let me think about it."

"It's your call, but *please* don't delay this. Time is of the essence."

"Yeah, ain't that the truth."

I shouldn't have hung up on Professor Hardy. I realised that even as was I doing it. But even she can't understand what it's like to really live with this disease. She gets the dying bit, obviously, but you have to live this thing to fully get the living bit.

Right now, at age twenty-four, the ripe old age of forty seems like a distant possibility. Non-CF people might say it's a lifetime away. CF people don't describe it that way, though.

21

The air in Karratha is rank this time of year. The monsoon's back further up north and it plays with our climate here like a cat with a mouse. No wonder people go troppo. It's got this certain pong and a thick heat that dominates every part of living here. Forty-plus degrees today. Just like yesterday, and tomorrow.

There are thunderstorms every second day, too. I'd never heard thunder like it when I first moved here, but I'm so used to it all now, I hardly even notice. The storms roll in off the desert and kinda stop south of Karratha. The locals have this theory that the iron in the ground here creates, like, a force field that holds the thunderheads back; but the indigenous people reckon there's a dreamtime turtle over the sky between Karratha and Port Headland that keeps the storms out.

But sometimes the big turtle, or the iron, or whichever it is, will lose the fight and a thunderstorm will do its thing right over the town. When it happens, it's time to grab a beer and head for the porch. And tonight, is one of those nights. Time to sit and gawk at the most super-intense light show on earth.

As my eyes adjust to the dim light of the yard, Allie's form emerges in the gloom for a millisecond as another lightning bolt flashes out towards the ocean. Her tall, thin shape is revealed in black silhouette as she stands near the edge of the back porch, just out of the rain.

I'm safely against the wall and out of the wet stuff, cold-kickin' it in a rusty deck chair. You quickly learn to avoid being under the edges of roofs up here, unless you want an instant shower. There's not a gutter or a drain in the world that could handle these downpours, so the builders in Karratha don't install them.

"So, tomorrow?" I ask.

"Yep," she answers.

"What time's your flight?"

"You know the deal. First FIFO jet lands, chopper leaves a half-hour later."

When she's in a contemplative mood, like this, her sentences are no longer than they need to be, which can make her seem ... snappy. But I'm learning to read her. The real her.

"Another two weeks, wow. You ever get tired of being out there?"

"Yeah, sometimes. But it pays the bills."

The silence is interrupted only by the raindrops bouncing off the corrugated roof. We still have these longish silences between us, but they're not really awkward. Not anymore.

"Guess I'll just work and play the Xbox," I whimper, "and do my physio and that stuff." And it's clear to me hear how pathetic it sounds even before I finish the sentence.

Allie waits a few seconds. "You know, Dylan, if you want to say, 'I'm going to miss you'," she says in a flat hush, "then why don't you just say it?"

Bugger it. Who's reading who?

"Um, well, yeah. I'll miss you. A bit," I mumble.

"Fish-tits! Is *that* the best you can do?"

"Well, are you gonna miss me?"

She shifts onto another foot. "I'll think about it while I'm away and give you the low down when I get back."

"So that's a *yes*, then."

There's silence again, like we'd said nothing. But the words I didn't say, the words I can't say, are tugging at my mind like a runaway train. I know I'll miss her. It's what happens when she's gone, no matter how much I convince myself otherwise. And I'm sure she misses me. But it's not the next two weeks I'm thinking about. It's next year, and every year after that.

What will Allie do when I'm gone?

I can't see Allie enough to read her right now, not in the dark. She's just this shadow out in the grey, and there's a wispy trail of something snaking up above her head into the night.

"That'll kill you," I say, all teacher-like.

"Piss off."

"Nice. You're always telling *me* what to do, but I can't even make a suggestion your way."

"Suggestion noted," she says, as she takes another puff.

"I would've thought you'd um … avoid that stuff?"

"*God*, can't I enjoy a ciggie in peace?"

"Nope. I'm your voice of God tonight," I say like a smart arse.

"Yeah, nah, I don't need any God. Thanks anyway."

Another roll of thunder booms around and past us. The kitchen windows shake and the porch roof vibrates.

"It's just … it worries me."

She huffs. "Why?"

"Well for one thing, smoke sets me off my coughing, and an ignition source anywhere near my little mate," I say, knocking on my oxygen bottle with my knuckles for effect, "could send both of us into orbit. So keep that crap well clear of me."

"Oh, *duh*, I get all that. And you know I never smoke close to you."

"Yeah, but anything that can damage someone's lungs, it, um, it gets me thinking."

Another huff. "You done now?"

I'm on a roll, though. These words need to be said. "I read somewhere that emphysema is a bit like CF, or even bad COVID, at the end."

"Chillax, dude. I haven't got those."

I lean back and grip my hands behind my head. "But you could, like, get really sick down the track."

Allie flicks the red-glowing butt to the ground, snuffs it out with a foot, and leans back against a porch-upright, arms crossed. "Free country."

"Suppose so. Your choice."

"Exactly," she snaps.

"So, if I'm gonna die of something that's nuking my lungs—this frickin disease which I have no control over—then why-the-hell would you choose to damage yours?"

She shrugs. "Hey, YOLO, remember? A bus could hit me tomorrow. Whatever's gonna get me, will get me."

"Oh, right. So who's the fatalist now?"

"You been googling again? Who cares what happens to me."

"I care," I blurt.

"Why?" she says.

"We're … mates."

Her head snaps around to face me.

"Enough said," I add in a whisper.

And it is. Good mates has to be enough. Anything further or deeper or closer becomes too dodgy. All too hard and too awful when the other person leaves, whatever the circumstances might be. And that's not going to happen to me, not again. And there's no way I'll ever allow it to happen to her.

Allie stays facing me for a few seconds, not moving and not saying another word, before she turns to face the dark garden again. There're two flashes of lightning in quick succession. Enough illumination to see her black silhouette lighting up her next cigarette, and another line of smoke begin its steady upwards climb.

22

My desk phone buzzes, again. I've got the ringtone on zero so no-one in the office can hear it, and I've switched my mobile to vibrate.

I've got work to do.

I'm only in the office a few hours a day now. Some days I can't make it in at all. I'm losing the control I used to have over the coughing fits, and I get breathless and light-headed and can't talk that much. The oxygen tank and tube are with me 24/7. I'd be lost without those things. Might even be dead.

But now the office lady has come from downstairs. It's game over, clearly.

"Dylan!"

No choice but to look up.

"Why aren't you answering your phone?" she barks. "There's a Professor Hardy who's called reception. Says she's been trying to call but you won't pick up."

"Right," I say. "Sorry."

I take my mobile out to the foyer and find Professor Hardy in my contacts. She's the last person I want to talk to. I haven't got the voice or the time to waste on her hassling me to move back to Perth.

Out of ear, out of mind.

"Professor Hardy," the voice says when the line connects.

"Hey. It's Dylan."

"Thank goodness. Where have you been? We've been trying to call you."

"Been busy. Whazzup?"

Her lecture is coming and I brace myself to hear it, again. All the reasons I have to ditch my life and career here. All the logic about why Perth is the only place to be. About why CF is everything, and everything else is nothing.

"Dylan," she says. "You have a lung donor. We have a match."

The walls spin at a wonky angle and the floor goes to mush.

"Dylan? Dylan? You there?"

"Sort of."

"I know this comes as a shock. It often does. But this is the best news you'll ever receive. We're in the right window of time for this procedure. This is your chance."

"Yep."

"We need to get you to Perth, now."

Perth?

I look back into the office. Colleagues are busy tapping away at their keyboards, some are having casual chats, others talking on phones. Alan's in conversation with someone in the corridor. This is *my* place. This is the place I've transformed, and it's the place that's transformed me. I belong here.

This is where I am.

My next words fall out of me with no thought. "I … I dunno."

Professor Hardy snaps, and her voice flips into something like I've never heard. "*Don't be ridiculous.* Many CF patients don't even get this chance. You *must* take this."

I take a big breath in and rub my eyes. "What … um, what will happen?"

"The transplant surgery must begin in the next twelve hours. We have to get you on a plane and into the hospital. You must get here tonight. Every minute counts."

"I'll um—"

"Dylan!"

"I'll get back to you," I say, and hang up the call.

··········

A world in a cubicle?

This tiny space is like an old mate. I recognise every fitting, each wall surface, each screw in the lining, every scratch of graffiti. The dim vibe and the dank ceiling above are my old friends. It's the place where I hurl, or explode, or both, when I need to. Yep, this cubicle is my home away from home at work.

Alan's voice echoes out in the wash area. "Dylan. *Dylan.* Are you in there, mate?" He's thumping on the cubicle door like my life depends on it.

If I hold my eyes shut tight, real tight, maybe he'll go away.

My mobile won't stop vibrating.

"Dylan, please!"

And then a scuffling noise above me, and gymnastic huffs and grunts which tell me someone other than Alan is climbing the cubicle wall. I don't want to look up, but I do.

A familiar face stares down at me. "Hey, mate."

"Hey."

Greg looks bizarre draped over the cubicle partition above me, but his overdone smile seems somehow reassuring.

"Time to c'mon out. You're a popular fella, and we can't keep the fans waiting."

....

"Yep, yep, right *now*. I don't give a flying fark what the procedure is, just do it." And he slams his phone down. This is an agitated Alan like I've never seen. He looks up at me. "Right. That's organised, and Greg's bringing his car around. Let's go."

"Go where?"

Alan thrusts a hand in the air, pleading. "The *airport*. Where else?"

"No, no, I—"

"Enough of your gibberish. There's one last plane going to Perth tonight and you're going to be on it. A Flying Doctor plane can't get here in time, so there's no other choice."

I shake my head like a nutcase.

This can't be happening.

But Alan's not finished. "What the hell is wrong with you? Professor Hardy told me you *have* to be there in a few hours, so there's no time to waste. You gotta fly down or you'll..." His voice tapers off, losing its newfound ballsy vibe.

"Or I'll what?"

"Or you'll die," Greg adds as he strides into the room.

There's a need for me to say something, now. Something decisive, and defensive, and profound. *Anything*.

But no words come.

Greg grabs my oxygen bottle with one hand and pulls it vertical, ready to roll out the door. He picks up the nasal tube with his other hand. "Thing is," he says as he folds the tube over into a sharp kink, "if you don't get out of that *bloody* chair and into my car, I'm going to hold this here until you pass out. Then we'll carry your sorry arse onto the plane ourselves. Your choice."

••••••••••

I think I got up and went with Greg and Alan to the car, but I don't remember, not really. The whole thing was like watching a streaming doco when you're on the edge of sleep. Kinda real, and kinda not.

And my bloody mobile won't stop buzzing in my pocket.

23

"Mr Malloy," the flight attendant says with a smile, "we've given you the whole front row on this side. We hope you'll be comfortable."

"Thanks," I wheeze. "Hey, call me Dylan."

This is still a dream. Flashes of racing past airport check-in. Alan speaking loudly to someone at the gate. A vague awareness of being handled through the door and out across the tarmac in the driving rain and thick heat. Greg dragging my oxygen bottle behind me, soaked to his skin. A gate attendant trying his best to hold an umbrella over us in the wind. Alan rushing forward to the stairs with some papers.

And now it's me sitting alone as the other passengers come on board. Some stare as they go past and their looks tell me what their mouths don't: *why does he get to board first?* Or: *poor bugger, he looks near death.*

My phone buzzes again and I slide it out my pocket to turn the frickin thing off. But I check my snap messages out of habit to find thirty-two of them bold and unread. Nearly all from Allie:

Allie: got a message from the doc! get to airport!!!

Allie: you there? PLEASE call or msg me

Allie: im going 2 try fly back. … i'll pull favours

On and on the messages went, most of them similar. Until the final ones:

Allie: Will be on last chopper out. … hope 2 be there in time. … c u on plane

Allie: flying will be okay, I'll be with you

I go to shoot off a snap reply.

"I'm sorry, sir. All devices now need to be turned off or in flight-mode," the flight attendant says with the same smile as before.

"I just have to—"

"*No*, sir. We're running late. Please switch it off."

And she watches me until I do.

…………

There's only about a hundred passengers on the 737 and no one else is boarding, but the front cabin door is still wide open and the airstairs are still in place.

After a few minutes, I hear someone race up the metal steps. A young man in uniform bursts in. He pulls off his hi-vis jacket, shakes his hair free of water and takes a breath. The guy looks soaked, and I notice three gold bars on each of his shoulders as he turns left and heads for the cockpit door. Things are coming back. It makes sense; the first officer gets the raw end of the deal and has to do the pre-flight walk-around, no matter the weather. Poor bugger. He punches four numbers into a keypad, opens the cockpit door, and disappears into the secret world of pilot-business.

But the front cabin door is still open. Why?

The ramp-guy has already rushed in and out with the load sheet.

The cabin crew seem peeved and impatient.

More heavy footsteps, now. More wet people. Two men in uniform and a beefy guy struggling to walk thanks to the metal cuffs around his wrist and ankles and a chain linking in between.

The beefy guy sits in my row on the opposite side of the aisle. One of the uniform guys—a cop by the looks of him—sits on the aisle seat next to him. The other cop says something and leaves. He's barely outside when a flight attendant heaves the cabin door shut and locks it.

As the sound of the air conditioning dies overhead, the thought hits me: this is happening. This frickin flight is actually happening.

And Allie hasn't made it here in time.

24

It's all coming back. All the stuff I used to love. All the stuff I now detest. Every sight, every sound; every movement, texture, and scent as the crew prepare this plane for departure.

And I have to fight off every one of those things. I must fight them in my mind. I must stand guard and make sure those bastard sensations don't get lodged in my brain. I've been able to push down almost all thoughts of my mum until now. I've been able to avoid the image of her sitting in an airline seat like this one, on her final flight. Her excitement as they got underway. Her longing for home, and for me.

But, now. Here. Here in this bloody jet, those painful thoughts seem to be winning.

"Sir, your seatbelt?"

"Oh, yeah." I curse at making such a rookie error. I snap the thing in. She smiles and moves to row two.

As I go to sit back, the beefy guy in the opposite window seat is sitting forward, and he looks over at me. He gives me a gross smirk and flicks his head up in a show of disgust. "Retard," he snorts, scorning at the oxygen bottle next to me.

I lift my arms and make a big show of how free they are as I rub my wrists and forearms with each opposite hand. I give his handcuffs and chain the best death stare I can muster, then wink at him and sit back out of his view.

But it's okay. There's a big cop with a gun between the guy and me.

So, whatever, Mr prison dude.

The dull drone of the left engine picks up speed as the start cycle engages. I anticipate the exact moment the pilots will flick the engine start lever upwards and bring that CFM-56 to full roaring life.

Once a plane geek, always a plane geek. The flicker of the cabin lights tells me the pilot has switched generator power from the Auxiliary Power Unit to the two engines. I feel the wheel brakes release and we taxi out of our apron parking spot and hang a hard right turn. The 'cabin crew be seated for departure' call comes across the intercom, followed by two *dings* of the seatbelt sign as we taxi like a bat out of hell for the runway. There's the whir of the flaps being extended as the last of the flight attendants makes it back to her crew seat at the front.

We don't even stop at the runway hold-point. We're straight onto the runway and the engines are spooling up to take-off thrust as we lurch around the corner to line up.

The flight attendant finishes strapping herself in, looks at her watch, and winces. This plane is running late, that's for sure.

The edge lights are flicking past as we race down the runway. I shut my eyes as I feel the jet lift-off and free itself of the earth. The landing gear retracts with a loud whir and a thud, like a gentle kick up my arse.

My eyes remain shut as I throw some sleeping pills in my mouth and force them down my throat. I ignore the sounds and vibrations of the plane as it climbs, battling on with my unwanted thoughts, and hoping like hell for the relief of sleep.

What might I dream? Of flying? About my mum? Or the operation I'm supposed to be having tonight?

I take another good swig of oxygen through the nose cannulas and settle back. This flight will take at least two hours and I'll take whatever comes.

••••••••••••

The single *ding* as the seatbelt sign goes off sounds distant, like an echo through a long tunnel. It tells me we're climbing through eleven thousand feet.

The weightless warmth of the hazy border between consciousness and sleep washes through me. And a sensation of falling. Falling gently, in slow, rhythmic waves.

And then—

25

It's like the tide coming in. One minute you can sense those warm waves of sleep washing over you. At a specific point—a point you can never put your finger on—all the usual sights and sounds of being conscious go mute. As if you're slipping underwater but not at all worried about being there. You're held submerged by the gentle sleep of an ocean of nothing without a care in the world.

And afterwards, it's like the tide going out. Part of you becomes exposed above the surface. Light, vibrations, and sensations return. You sense the waves of sleep ebb away, and suddenly you're lying exposed on the sand.

You're awake.

Although, there's also that millisecond when you think you might be awake but you're not really sure. Like, am I here? Am I still dreaming? Or in my case, am I *in* my nightmare?

It's dark outside and the plane's cabin is really dim.

The cop and his beefy prisoner are both heads back and fast asleep.

My head's throbbing. Bit dizzy. Vision seems off.

My brain struggles to make sense of what my wristwatch is showing. We've been airborne for over an hour and I really need to piss. Time to make for the loo at the front of the plane, a few steps from my seat.

Not sure why, but we're bumping along in this turbulence and the flight crew don't seem to care. They'll usually try to climb or turn out of it. But not these guys, they must be really keen to get home.

Glad I choose to sit down for this loo manoeuvre. If I'd stood up to pee, this tiny toilet space would have copped the worst of it. I wash my hands while bracing myself against the bumps, then ease myself out the door with my bottle in tow.

The cabin is still dim and for a moment my eyes play a trick.

There's a pair of feet lying horizontal on the floor.

Idiot. Get a grip.

As I go past the narrow galley space, I see her: the smiling flight attendant. The one who told me to turn off my phone and do up my seatbelt. It's not unusual to see a flight attendant in a galley, mind you. You expect to see them working there mid-flight. But I didn't expect to see her lying on the floor with her head leaning crooked against a drinks cart.

And there's those horizontal feet again. They belong to her.

Huh?

Panic. Chest heaves. Throat dry. Rip away my nasal tube, ditch the oxygen tank, and drop to my knees. Grab her by the shoulders and shake. Gentle at first, then more and more vigorous as it becomes clear she isn't responding. Her head slips off the cart and hits the floor with a dull thump. This woman is out like a light.

Think, dickhead!

You're still asleep, obviously. You thought you'd dream a nightmare and here you are right in the thick of it.

Up now and in the aisle. This dream is better than any 3D virtual reality I've ever experienced. I can still feel the floor under my shoes and the texture of the headrests on my hands as I walk the aisle, doing my best to stay upright in the turbulence. The usual odours in an airliner cabin are there, although some wafts of odour seem … off.

The cop and the prisoner are still right out to it: heads back, fast asleep. Yellow oxygen masks are dangling above them.

What?

Row two. Empty. But oxygen masks there too.

Row three. More oxygen masks and an old couple on the left. She's head on the window and off with the fairies. He's slouched half across her. That can't be comfortable.

Row four. A mum and two kids. One curled up next to her. The other rolled up on her lap. She's staring ahead at her seat back, eyes wide and fixed, like she's watching the best rom-com of her life. But there's no screen there.

A big guy on the other side—aisle seat. Head forward, crumpled over like an abandoned Ken doll.

Row five. Empty, but still the masks.

Row six. Four FIFO workers still dressed in their hi-viz. All asleep. Two leaning heads together. Almost romantic.

Huh?

Row seven. Young couple on the right—out to it and stooped forward against their seat belts. Heads wobbling to the turbulent jolts. The young guy's face is whiter than a wedding cake.

Row eight. Empty.

Row nine. Old guy, head back. Asleep? No. His eyes are wide open. But what's he staring at? Something's off here. I wave some fingers between his eyes and whatever he's looking at on the ceiling. No reaction. Nothing. Grab a shoulder. Shake. Gentle. Then hard. His head falls forward and his stare continues at the floor. And his lips are, like … blue.

Damn. Some frickin' nightmare, this is. Full colour and all?

Look up now. Past row ten, and eleven, and all the way to the end of the cabin. There's an insane forest of yellow oxygen masks bouncing away in the turbulence. And there, right at the end of the aisle, there's another pair of legs on the floor of the rear galley. Also horizontal. Also still.

Head's swimming. Vision narrow and blurry. The panic is still there, but so is this sensation of almost excitement? It's like I want to giggle but I don't understand why. There's nothing funny in this nightmare scene. Nothing at all.

What the hell's happening to me?

I go back for my oxygen bottle and grab for my nasal tube. Three big breaths followed by the usual wet cough attack. More sucks on the oxygen and my head clears a bit and the tingling in my fingers eases.

As I turn towards the front of the plane, there's a colossal thump as the plane heaves and drops in a big hit of turbulence, and—

26

It's not like the tide. Waking up from being unconscious is not like waking up from sleep, and especially when the first sensation you get is a throbbing pain that stabs right through your head.

The bottom edge of my oxygen bottle is filling my view. *Why*? And there's this dampness under my head, on the carpet. I pull a reluctant arm into service and get some fingers to the damp. It's warm, and dark red.

Blood? Mine?

Shit!

Dreaming I'd woken up within a nightmare was one thing. But going unconscious, regaining consciousness, and *still* being in the same nightmare? No, not possible.

As I pull myself up, gripping the top of a seat, the surrounding scene confirms it. The old guy is still staring at the floor, eyes wide open, and his lips are even bluer now.

A voice in my head puts me straight: *this is no nightmare, this is happening*.

But what is happening? Why are all these people so fast asleep or unconscious and why won't they respond?

My brain races away as I move down the aisle shaking people. I shout at them. "Hey! Hey mate, wake up!" They stare or keep sleeping. In the end I scream as loud as my pathetic lungs will go, "Is anyone on this plane awake?"

Nothing. Everyone's still out to it.

Except for me.

Or…?

I tear down the aisle and thump into the cockpit door. I bang on it with everything I've got. "Open up, *please.* Can anyone hear me in there?"

I yell over and over, bashing away with both fists, till my energy drains and I fall in an exhausted heap on the floor. But there's no movement from the cockpit. No sound at all from in there. There's only the constant hum of the engines and the creaks and groans of the cabin as the plane reacts to more hits of turbulence.

••••••••••

So this is it. This is how it ends?

I've heard people say when they realise they're about to die, they get this strange sense of peace, like a resignation waiting for an end.

So I'll sit here on the floor with my back against the cockpit door and wait for that peace to wash in and make everything alright. I could just laugh to myself as the plane runs out of fuel and goes down in silence? Maybe the peace will be enough to cancel the terror as we spiral for the ground?

But, as more minutes slip by, it's not coming. I can't sense any frickin peace. Not even a hint.

There's another emotion, though. I feel like running, or fighting, or something. As if there's more to be done, as if I've got some say in how this whole shit-show might play out?

My eyes turn to the ceiling, don't know why. There's the plain beige of the cabin ceiling in the dim wash of the LED lights and a bright green *EXIT* sign. A wall panel to my right is interrupted by a square box halfway down. It's a panel with numeric keys.

As I inhale another big one through my nasal tube, my scrambled brain finally registers: that panel is the keypad for the lock on the cockpit door.

··········

More minutes slip away before things fully register. More big breaths on the oxygen seem to help, although the *O_2 20%* remaining indicator on the bottle is becoming a worry.

I'm not much good at maths, but I'm pretty good at remembering numbers. When the first officer went into the cockpit before we took off, I saw the four numbers he punched into the keypad.

I'm pressing those numbers right now: *7…3…7…8.*

It's hard to believe they use the model number of the plane as their security code, but there you go. It's the equivalent of using 'password' as your password.

And this security system is all so simple. No fancy surveillance camera and remote door release on this old plane.

The little keypad beeps and a light flashes green.

There's a metallic click.

I put a hand on the cockpit door handle, gulp, and pull.

There, before me now, is the world of airline pilots in all its mesmerising complexity.

27

First thing I notice is the captain in the left seat. The seat is slid back and to the left on its rails, as if she was about to get up. But she's slouched on the seat and leaning hard left with her shoulder up against the side panel. Her head's skewed unnaturally on the glass of the side window, as if she's trying hard to look past the nose of the plane, but with her eyes shut.

The first officer in the right-hand seat must have been in control. His seat is forward and his safety harness is on. He's slouched forward against the straps with his arms dangling useless by his sides. His head's hanging forward in space near the control column and bouncing stupidly with each bump of turbulence. The poor guy looks like a ventriloquist's doll having a seizure.

I don't bother shaking either of the pilots. The captain isn't breathing and the first officer's lips and nose are a clear shade of blue. CPR is not a possibility 'coz I'll only end up heaving and spluttering. There's no such thing as the cough of life.

So, I'm standing behind them now, wondering what the hell to do. There's a constant beeping sound going off, like a warning or something. On instinct, I scan across the displays on the main instrument panel and the mode control panel above. They're all there, all those things in the cockpit I used to know so well. But it's not the same. These things before me are real and in three dimensions. I'm used to seeing them on flat screens and virtually 'touching' them with a mouse pointer. This is different. Really different.

And I feel like an impostor. I shouldn't be here, and the very thought of being the only person conscious on this plane is gripping me harder with every breath.

The panting and wheezing and dizziness is coming back. I lower myself backwards, knowing the jump seat is there to catch me, deflating there as my guts tighten and my brain locks-up.

I should not be here.

This can't be happening.

No idea what to do.

And that sense of peace—the peace for the end—is nowhere.

....

Not sure how long I've been sitting here. Seconds? Minutes? Time's lost its grip.

But the plane, at least, is still awake. An orange MASTER CAUTION light has illuminated on the captain's side, along with a FUEL fault indicator light.

Fuel?

My eyes go to the digital fuel gauges in the centre display. The left and right wing tanks are showing one thousand, three hundred kilograms each. The centre tank is showing zero.

Zero?

My eyes race to the overhead panel above me. Scan left and down looking for the fuel panel ... and *there*. The switch layout is familiar and I'm drawn to the annunciator lights for the centre tank fuel pumps, which are glowing a concerned orange. The pilots must have been using the centre fuel tank, but somewhere during the flight, probably after they passed out, the fuel in the tank's been all used up.

I know what to do, I think.

But do I? Should I?

My hand reaches up for the switches while my brain is still arguing with itself. My fingers grab the left pump switch. I pull it back a fraction to release it, and move it to the *OFF* position. I do the same with the right pump switch.

With a lean forwards, I press the *MASTER CAUTION* button on the glareshield. The plane is happily pumping fuel from just the two wing tanks now, so the *FUEL* warning and *MASTER CAUTION* lights have nothing more to complain about. Both lights extinguish and go blank, and the irritating beeping has stopped too.

So far so good?

But before I sink back to the jump seat to consider my little victory, other lights have got my attention. There's three lights in the left-side window and they aren't moving in tandem with this cockpit. Are they outside? A flashing red light blinks above, a steady white one seems nearer, and there's an orange glow further back.

I stare hard but can't make it out. Might be reflections?

Suddenly, all three lights twist and warp. Whatever that thing is, it's definitely outside, and bigger and closer now.

There's a flash. A white light streaks out nearby. It bounces back from the cloud layers we're skimming between and fills the surrounding blackness with brilliant white. The source of the light is real close—forward and left of the cockpit. I can't see the object very well, but it's not long before a distinctive shape, silhouetted hard against the white light now surrounding the plane, becomes clear.

It's a fighter jet. An F35 Lightning-II with its ice lights on, shining ahead.

I freeze. How am I supposed to react? It's good there's another living, conscious person up here with me. But he's not really here. He's *out there*. It's only me in here.

The F35 slides further right and back. It's super close now. The pilot has lit up his cockpit and the shape of his helmet is visible, I can see he's twisted around and looking in my direction. The pilot's hands are moving up, down, pointing, signalling. He's getting really excited as he points at me, then at his helmet, then downwards; but I can't work out what he's trying to tell me.

I try to signal back but I don't think he can see me that well.

His signals become more crazed before he shakes his head and turns away. In an instant, the F35 rolls hard left and flies out of sight.

And that's when I see them. The weapons bay doors on the underbelly of the F35. Only for a second, but long enough to comprehend those doors are open and the weapons bay is not empty.

28

What are the chances?

What are the chances the son of a woman who was in an airliner destroyed by a surface-to-air missile, is himself—years later—in an airliner destroyed by an air-to-air missile launched by an RAAF F35?

You couldn't make this stuff up. The chances might seem minuscule in theory, but right now the probability of me getting blown out of the sky is looking pretty strong.

Do these pricks think I'm a terrorist?

But there's nothing I can do. Seems I *am* a fatalist, after all.

I stare at the captain's flight controls and swallow hard. The column and yoke seem to hang alone in space and every now and then they move slightly as the autopilot adjusts things. The very thought of putting my hands anywhere near those controls stabs me with a freezing shiver. Pushing a button and moving a switch is one thing, but *flying*? *Me*? And Nancy's words from years ago have started echoing between my ears: '*... if you don't take control when those opportunities are put right in front of you...*'

Then I realise: there's another variable in this whole equation.

Me.

Stuff happens now before I'm even conscious of my decisions. I've somehow dragged the captain's body off the pilot seat and plonked her on the jump seat. I'm sitting on her seat now and in the forward position with those flight controls right in front of me. The headset is squeezed over my head and onto my ears. Thin microphone boom at my lips.

My eyes search for the radio transmit switch as my ears take in the radio chatter. The air traffic controller is talking with other planes, and sometimes when there's a break in the radio traffic, she transmits, "Jet-west two-three-eight, Jet-west two-three-eight, Melbourne Centre if you read this transmission, *ident.*"

Might be for us? Must be our callsign?

The F35 is still nowhere to be seen. Probably behind us? I gotta get a transmission out. *Now.*

Still searching. The audio panel next to me looks confusing as hell and I've never used one for real. Forget that. My fingers feel across the two arms of the control yoke. There, under my index finger, must be the transmit button?

Nothing for it. I press and hold the button.

But … what do I say?

No words come.

I let the transmit button go, like a complete loser, as if it just gave me 240 volts.

"Last aircraft transmitting, nothing heard," the controller says, deadpan.

I jump in the seat, heart now racing hard.

Me?

Yes, you, dickhead. It's like Allie's in the other seat.

Press again. "Ah, this is … Jet-West two-three-eight," I manage in a broken whisper.

I let go of the transmit button. Feels like I've launched something terrible, or broken some rule, or something.

"Last aircraft calling, say again callsign?"

Jeez, she heard me.

"Ah, it's Jet-West two-three-eight."

"Jet-West two-three-eight, good to hear from you. Confirm all ops normal?"

"Um, yes. But no, not really."

"Jet-West two-three-eight. Say again? Confirm ops normal?"

"We're ah … we're okay, I think, but I'm not the pilot."

"Jet-West two-three-eight. Say again?"

"I'm … I'm just a passenger."

The radio goes silent for ten long seconds.

"Jet-West two-three-eight. Sir, you need to put a crew member on the radio, now."

"I would, but, they can't."

More silence, and static. The other pilots on frequency have stopped talking, too.

A deep male voice eventually punches into my headset, "Jet-West two-three-eight, I'm a supervisor with Melbourne Centre. Please confirm, you are a passenger?"

"Yes."

"Where is the flight crew?"

"They're here, but, they're not conscious. I think the captain might be dead."

Another pause that feels like forever.

"Jet-West two-three-eight. State your intentions."

Shit, they really *do* think I'm a terrorist?

"Hang on, wait," I plead. "I don't understand what's going on here. This is not my doing. I just want to get out of this."

The supervisor sounds pissed. "How did you get into the cockpit?"

"I, ah … the door was open."

More silence tells me this guy isn't buying my pathetic lie.

"Jet-West two-three-eight, put a cabin crew member on the radio. *Now.*"

"I can't. They're all unconscious. I think all the other passengers are too."

"Everyone on the plane is unconscious, except you? Is that what you're telling me?" he insists.

"That's what it looks like."

The other controller comes back on. "Jet-West two-three-eight, okay, standby. We are running out of range on this frequency and need you to change. Somebody will come on in a second to talk you though how to switch the radio over to 129.5."

"I can do that, contact 129.5."

And as I hit the transfer switch to change the COM1 radio frequency to *129.50*, I realise how smart-arsed my response must have sounded.

But, whatever. "Melbourne Centre, Jet-West two-three-eight on one-two-nine decimal five," I announce.

Another guy comes on. He sounds rushed and stressed. "Jet-West two-three-eight, this is Perth Approach. Are you a pilot?"

"No."

"What's your name?"

"Dylan. I'm Dylan Malloy."

"Ok. I'm Scott. I'm the air traffic supervisor with Perth Approach. How do you know how to work the radios, Dylan?"

"I don't, not really, but I used to do a lot of flight-simming as a kid. I'm only doing what I can remember."

"Ah, okay."

"This might sound dodgy, but believe me, it isn't. I've got no idea how I ended up in this freaked-out mess."

"It's okay, Dylan. Easy there. I'm here to help."

"Glad to hear it, 'coz I'm the only one here, and I didn't ask for this, and everyone's asleep, or unconscious, or dead, and there's an armed F35 out there somewhere, and I don't understand what the *fuck* is going on!"

"Dylan, Dylan," he says, his voice deliberately slow and calm. "Easy, mate. You've done good. Let's take this step-by-step."

But my brain is mush. Visions of mum, of planes, of missiles, of dead bodies, of fireballs, of white faces and blue lips, of things slamming into the ground. They're all playing through me like the worst edited movie ever made.

"Dylan, are you there? Dylan, talk to me?"

Another big inhale through my nasal prongs. My hands are trembling and I can't feel my legs. "I'm here," is all I can say, my voice wobbly.

"Okay, good. Just keep talking to me, yeah?"

"Okay."

His voice is deep and smooth and measured, like a late-night radio host doing love-song dedications. "We'll get you through this, Dylan. Stay with us."

His voice seems reassuring, but I can't make myself believe a word he's saying.

29

We'd spent the past five minutes going over things in the cockpit. Scott put another guy on the radio with him; a 737 check-and-training captain called Anderson, who they'd found at Perth Airport and brought in to help.

They've both asked me a stack of questions and I've been able to give them the answers, eventually. Some of the cockpit indications were tricky to find, but we got there.

"So, reconfirm for me," Anderson says, "the three annunciations at the top of your primary flight display. What are they indicating?"

"Okay, from the left—N1, then L-NAV, then ALT."

"Right. Good. And it's displaying C M D right above the artificial horizon?"

"Yep."

"Great. The aircraft is stable on autopilot. It's been tracking the planned flight route, but it's obviously still in climb mode, even though it's levelled off."

"Yeah. Looks that way."

"Scott tells me you know a bit about flying, so I'll tell you things as we figure them out. We've verified Melbourne Centre gave the flight crew an initial climb limit of twenty-four thousand feet out of Karratha, so the autopilot has levelled off at that altitude, which is much lower than their planned cruise altitude of thirty-seven thousand."

"Yep, I understand."

"Which explains the very high rate of fuel burn," he says.

The worry in Anderson's words is clear. My eyes return to the digital gauges showing seven hundred and fifty kilograms of fuel remaining in each of the two wing tanks. The 737 burns about one thousand two hundred kilos per engine, per hour, and my brain does the math even before I tell it to.

Bugger it.

"We aren't going to make it, are we?"

There's a few seconds of nothing before Anderson responds, "Let's not worry about that for now, we're going to—"

My ears switch off. He's full of crap.

My eyes go down to the flight management computer beside my right knee. The bottom line of the FMC's display screen has a simple message for me in all-caps: INSUFFICIENT FUEL.

"If only Anderson could read this now," I whisper to myself.

But the usefulness of this FMC thing is something I can still remember, and I reckon it can help me out. So I press the CLR key to get rid of the fuel message, then press the PROG key to bring up the *Flight Progress* page on the screen. It displays a list of flight plan waypoints all the way to our destination.

The next waypoint is called TOPIR, and the FMC says it's eighty miles away. YPPH, or Perth airport, is further down the screen at the end of the list. The FMC is telling me Perth is '325' miles to go and there's a fuel prediction displayed too—'0.0'.

"Dylan? Dylan, do you read?" cuts into my ears and through my scrambling logic.

I shake my head and hit the transmit switch. "The FMC predicts we'll run out of fuel before Perth. So cut the crap, okay."

"Look," he manages eventually, "just stop fiddling with the FMC."

But my ears switch off again as my brain goes nuts. With fifteen hundred kilos of fuel left, we'll go maybe three hundred more miles before the engines cut out, if we're lucky, and that's allowing for a low-power descent too. Which means we'll be about thirty miles short of the airport.

I scan the navigation display. A blue airport symbol labelled *YGEL* is coming up out to our west. "Geraldton," I say on the radio. "Can we land there?"

"Dylan, let *us* work the plans."

"Easy for you to say. You're not the one up here about to bloody die. Now, can we land this thing at Geraldton, or not?"

"Sorry, no. We don't have the emergency services on the ground there to handle a major… (*click*)".

I wait a second, then finish his sentence for him, "…to handle a major crash, you mean?"

"Sorry. We do have to allow for that possibility."

"Jeez, mate. Can I say how *confident* you're making me feel."

"Sorry," he replies, deadpan. "Standby."

"What about the RAAF base; the one near Perth?"

"RAAF Pearce. No. It's out of the question. Give me a minute."

••••••••••

A minute?

What's a minute? What's an hour?

A minute to sit here listening to the dull roar of the air as it blasts past the plane's nose. A minute to resist staring at the grey-faced first-officer next to me. His head is still bouncing over his control column, his drool reaching down to it like stalactites growing in fast motion. A minute to watch the fuel remaining numbers steadily ticking downwards.

"Dylan," tingles in my headset.

"What?"

"Up on the forward overhead panel. The pressurisation panel. Can you see it?"

I look up. "Yeah. Yep, I think so."

"Okay. Look at the cabin altitude gauge in the centre. Tell me what altitude it's showing."

"Right. The needle's pointing to near the twenty."

"Twenty? Are you sure?"

"Yes."

"And the pressurisation mode switch to the right. Tell me what it's set to."

"The switch is set to MANUAL."

"Are you sure?"

"Yes of course I'm sure. What is this, a frickin trial?"

Scott's voice cuts in, "Easy mate. We're trying to work out what's happening. Captain Anderson has to be certain of these things."

Anderson continues, "That pressurisation mode switch, turn it to AUTO."

"Done," I say.

"Dylan, how are you feeling? How's your breathing?"

"Oh, so, you know about me, then?"

"Know about what?"

"About my cystic fibrosis."

"Sorry, mystic fibro what? I have no clue what that is."

"Join the club. But long story short, my lungs are screwed and I'm on an oxygen bottle till I get new ones. That's why I'm headed to Perth, apparently."

There's a long silence on the radio. I can sense air pressure building in the cockpit, and a gnawing ache is building in my ears.

"Dylan," Anderson says, "long story short from our end. Your oxygen bottle has probably kept you alive in more ways than one. It appears the pilots missed a critical checklist action before takeoff, which meant the aircraft cabin did not pressurise properly as the plane climbed out of Karratha. This also affects the oxygen level in the cabin, so everyone on board, except for you, has been starved of oxygen. They would have faded out of consciousness before anyone realised what was happening. It's called hypoxia."

"The pilots too?"

"Yes. Them too."

"What can I do? How do I get them awake?"

"There's nothing you can do other than restore cabin pressure, which is happening now. Given the fuel situation, we can only get the plane safely on the ground as quick as we can. The passengers and crew will get medical attention then."

He stops talking and I get a few seconds to think.

Another glance down at my oxygen bottle. My little mate, the oxygen bottle, that just saved my life. It's showing ten percent remaining in bright red flashing numbers.

30

More radio silence.

They're trying to work stuff out. I get that. It's not every day these guys would have a sixty-five tonne jet with no pilots and almost no fuel approaching a capital city airport. Sucks to be them.

And I'm working stuff out too. My eyes are going over the flight route on the navigation display. The magenta line leads from our position all the way to Perth, but there's a big dog-leg in the route. Dog-legs mean distance, and distance means we'll use more fuel.

My fingers are working the FMC keyboard again and I can barely believe what they're doing. Are they mine? With a few presses I select *YPPH*—Perth—and move it to the top of the flight plan. The EXEC key lights up. The system's asking me: *do ya really wanna do this?*

Yes, system. *I do*. I press the EXEC key and the dog-leg disappears from the navigation display. The autopilot commands a new heading and I sense the 737 roll to the right to capture it.

Sweet. It's like I remember.

Scott's right onto me. "Dylan, my scope shows your heading shifted right fifteen degrees."

"Yep."

And that's got Anderson interested. "What happened?" he barks.

"We're direct to Perth now," I reply. "No wasted miles. Less fuel to burn."

"What the hell! He can't be doing things like that. He's *not* a bloody pilot."

Silence.

I reckon Anderson has just realised he kept his transmit button down during his little side rant to Scott.

Scott's voice breaks the long silence. "Dylan? Dylan, do you copy?"

"Yeah, I copy alright," I say, pausing, "You *are* a pilot, Captain Anderson, I get that. But you're not the pilot *up here,* are you? It's not your guts gonna be spread all over some West Australian paddock."

Anderson's voice is tight now. "No more surprises. Okay? You know a bit, but only enough to get yourself into a lot of trouble. Only do what I say. Nothing more."

"U-g-g-h, roger," I say in the thickest, most sarcastic airline-pilot-sounding voice I can conjure. I pay for it, though. I break into another coughing fit that goes and goes, and goes.

The oxygen bottle readout clicks down to eight percent.

"Dylan, we're going to slow you down to give us more time. Now do exactly as I say."

"Yep."

"On the mode control panel, below where the speed setting is displayed, click the SPD button."

"Done."

"Good. What's the speed setting say?"

"Ah, it's three-two-zero."

"Okay, rotate the speed knob until the number reduces to two-seven-zero."

"Got it. Done."

The autothrottle system eases the thrust levers back, and our airspeed winds down to the new target airspeed of two hundred and seventy knots.

··········

For the next fifteen minutes I follow Anderson's every instruction. He steps me through the setup for the approach we'll be using into Perth—a straight-in approach from the north to runway 21 using the instrument landing system. We program it into the FMC and he talks me through how we'll conduct the descent and the approach.

I can handle those bits, I think. In fact, I'm feeling more confident by the minute.

Anderson's voice changes. Becomes more serious, like. "Then there'll be the landing. I'm going to be straight with you. This aircraft can't do a full auto-land into Perth, we don't have the right equipment for that."

"Right."

"The autopilot will get you lined up for the landing to the point when you're two hundred feet off the ground. From there, it will be up to you. You're going to have to take the controls and ease it onto the ground."

"So, when you say *ease it*, is that meant to make it sound easy?"

"Not really, no. Look. Conditions are pretty settled here. You won't have to do a lot. The main thing is to keep calm, execute the steps I give you, and don't over-control the plane."

"What could be easier?"

"Stop being a smart arse and listen. When you hear the GPWS system call 'three hundred', that means you're three hundred feet above runway altitude. This is when you'll transition from autopilot control to hand-flying the plane. You'll have your left hand on the control yoke, and your right hand on the thrust levers. Then you'll click the *Autopilot-disconnect* button on the yoke, and the *A/T-disconnect* buttons on the thrust levers to disconnect the autothrottle. You're the only one in control then." He pauses. "Still with me?"

I look down at those controls. My hands are there—trembling. "Yep."

"Keep your eyes on the far end of the runway. Use adjustments left and right on the yoke to keep the plane lined up with the centreline lights. You'll hear more altitude call-outs as you descend. When you hear 'fifty', ease the nose up slightly to slow the descent, but not to stop the descent. When you hear 'twenty', bring the thrust levers back to idle. Then, don't do a damn thing. Don't flare it. Just get the main wheels on the runway. The wheel brakes and the speed brakes on the wings will deploy automatically and bring you to a stop."

I get what Anderson's on about, sort of. The landing procedure was hazy in my memory, but it's coming back.

My head is near exploding, though. It's constantly switching between dread, euphoria, confusion, and limbo. And sometimes there's this tingly, giddy state where I feel like laughing. I've tried to joke with Anderson in some of those moments, and I don't understand why I'm even doing that. I bet he doesn't either.

And one minute I think *I got this*, the next I'm sure I'm gonna die. Still seems like a dream—a nightmare—and then something else happens in the cockpit and I realise again it's all too real.

My pathetic body isn't doing much better. Throat's tight. Legs not there again. Lungs on fire. Hands tremble. Damp spot in my pants.

But real or not, I've only got one chance at this. This is not a game. It's not even a simulation. I can't press pause and go take out the bins. And there's a hundred people back there beyond the cockpit door. Will they wake up now the oxygen is coming back to normal? I check the captain and first officer; they haven't moved and their grey colour doesn't fill me with hope.

"Dylan? You copy?"

"Ah, sorry, yep. I got it," I respond.

"Good. Now let's talk it through again."

I take a deep breath and listen like my life depends on it.

A quick look down.

O_2: 6% LOW.

Stick with me, little mate. Stick with me.

31

"Top of descent," I report on the radio.

We'd set an intercept altitude of two thousand feet for the final approach, and as the plane crosses TOD on the navigation display—the top of descent point—the autopilot eases the nose down and brings the thrust levers back towards idle. The altitude readout starts its countdown as the plane leaves twenty-four thousand feet and settles into a steady descent.

"Good. We can see you've begun the descent," Scott confirms.

Outside, up ahead, the tops of the cloud layer we've been skimming over are getting close. Grey and white puffs flick past, illuminated for a second by the plane's exterior lights, before I'm enveloped in the cloud and can't see a thing. It's strange blindly trusting all these systems in the dark, like I've got a blanket over my head and being led by around by a robot. Not that I have much choice.

"Dylan," Anderson's voice is curt. "Update me on the fuel."

I correct him. "*Please.*"

"Cut it out with the jokes."

I should remember, he's an airline pilot. Yeah, the humour centre in the brain, if there is one, isn't well developed. Maybe it wouldn't have been the right career for me after all? "Okay. Five-thirty kilos remaining each side," I report. "And I checked the FMC again. The fuel prediction is now one hundred kilos total when I land."

Those very words chill me out, and not in a good way. Not about the fuel, no, it's the 'when I land' bit that's completely hectic. Still, a part of me believes this all can't be happening.

"Good," he says. "We're in with a chance."

I'm thinking Anderson should probably give volunteering as a Lifeline phone counsellor a miss.

Yeah, stick to airline flying, old mate.

....

The sensation of being lost in the heavy blanket of cloud, of being completely enveloped, disappears. We're in the clear and the cloud layer is suddenly racing past above me. Out ahead, there's scattered dots of light in the blackness and an orange-white glow on the horizon: the city of Perth.

I hit the transmit button. "Passing eleven thousand and we've dropped below the cloud layer. Visual now."

"Right. Good. Things are going to happen pretty quick. Remember everything I've said. We'll do this one step at a time."

Anderson has gone over the descent, approach, and landing phases with me, in detail. Three times, I think. Might have been four. He's still sounding calm but there's a building tension in his voice. And he keeps rattling off the next things to do: "Landing lights on, engine start switches to continuous, altimeter to one-zero-three-zero."

"Checked."

"Your profile is looking good. It'll be idle-thrust all the way to two thousand feet."

The light out on the horizon is growing and brightening. The first signs of Perth's northern outskirts are creeping under the plane's nose and I can make out street lights and even car lights. Yeah, there's people on the ground, too.

No...

"I dunno," I stutter and cough again on the radio. "Is ah ... is this really a good idea?"

There's an awkward pause before Scott's voice comes in. "Yes it is. There's no other viable alternative, mate. If you were any other passenger up there, landing the plane probably wouldn't even be an option. This is a good idea because we've got *you*, Dylan. You can do this."

I'm shaking my head at nobody.

"This will work," he says.

I mumble, "I'll do my best."

"I know."

So I ask, "Is this the bit where Anderson is gonna tell me, 'I just want to say: good luck, we're all counting on you'?"

"If you come out of this in one piece," Anderson spits, his tone more animated and human-sounding for a change, "I'm personally going to *kick your arse*."

"Deal," I say. "And passing nine thousand feet."

"Copy that." His airline voice has returned. "Keep me up to date on your speed and rate of descent. We need to manage energy carefully."

"Okay. We're two-seventy knots, descending eighteen hundred feet a minute."

"Bring the speed target back to two-twenty, and you'll have stick out the boards to help reduce speed."

"The boards?"

"Sorry. Speed brakes. Handle's next to your right knee. Pull it up and back, but only about halfway back to the flight-detent."

....

"Through six thousand," I report. "Speed two-twenty, descending at sixteen hundred."

"Good. Return the speed brake handle to the down position, then lower the landing gear. The extra drag will help us manage the speed from here on."

I have to reach way over to my right for the landing gear lever. I tug at it, but it won't budge. "It won't move!" I yell on the frequency.

"Easy, Dylan. Pull the knob out first—it's on a spring—then move the handle to the down position."

The frickin thing suddenly responds and there's an epic kick in my seat and a roar from outside as the nosewheel drops below the cockpit floor. The three wheel lights flicker on the instrument panel, then hold steady.

"Phew. Gear down. Three greens."

"See what happens when you do exactly like I say?"

Arsehole.

"Set your speed for one-eighty knots," he continues, "and set flaps one."

I spin the speed setting down, then search for the flaps lever, beyond the thrust levers. *There.* I go to guide it back the '1' position but it won't move.

Damn it! But, maybe...?

I lift the flap handle upwards and it loosens and flicks into the slot.

"Flaps one," I report, trying to sound confident but probably sounding anything but.

32

O_2: 3% LOW

My little mate would yell that percentage at me if oxygen bottles could talk. But my breathing's settled a bit as we've got lower—we're passing five thousand feet now—and my head's clearer.

"Is the approach armed?" Anderson wants to know.

"Yep. APP light's on, and it's showing armed on my flight display."

"Good. It should capture the localiser and glideslope signals in about five miles. Set flaps to fifteen and set the speed to one-sixty-five knots."

My hands do as instructed. "Done."

"What's your fuel?"

"Two-fifty kilos."

"Okay. That'll have to do."

Great.

The sensation of speed is quite something, now. Up high, things on the ground seem to creep up towards the plane's nose and slip past at a nice easy rate. Down this low, everything is snapping past like it's all got somewhere to go. Buildings, street lights, freeways, houses, vehicle lights are everywhere and racing by too fast to comprehend. Further ahead, fifteen miles away, the lights of the airport are coming into view.

There's not much to do for the next minute, and the radio is quiet for a change. I think they're letting me take a breath before the final act of this shit-show really starts.

I go through the landing procedure in my head one more time. We've got everything set for the instrument landing system. The autopilot will capture the localiser to keep us lined up, and the glideslope will guide us down to the runway. Well, most of the way.

The altitude readout winds on down. 4600, 4500, 4400. Speed's steady and back to one-sixty knots. Rate of descent is steady.

We're set, I think.

Time is like, slowing or stretching or something. Or is that distance?

And I think I can feel it. A sense of peace?

Yeah, about goddamn time.

Seeing faces, now. People I've known. Flashes of memory. Aunt Cheryl. Allie. Nancy. Even Greg. And my mum. I squeeze my eyes shut for a second to flush those clips away. I've got no time for a life-in-review vid.

A different voice crackles in my headset. "Hey. It's Dylan, right?"

It's a steady male voice I don't recognise. "Ah, yeah. Who's this?" I transmit back.

"Talon-Two. Look outside, to your left."

My eyes search beyond the cockpit windows and above the mess of suburban lights and into the black of the sky. And again, the lights: a flashing red light blinks above, a steady white one is nearer, and there's an orange glow further back. This time I don't have to wonder what the object is.

The F35 pilot's turned his cockpit lighting up again. He's craned his head around hard to look at me. I can't see his face, but the shape of his sci-fi looking helmet is clear.

I don't know who 'Talon-Two' even is, and I hope the guy had a real name, once.

His voice echoes in my headset, thick and easy. "I'm a pilot," he says, "just like you."

I lift a hand to acknowledge him. I hope he can see it.

He lifts a gloved hand into view. He makes a fist and punches the air, like a call to attack, or something. I think I've been given a signal from a brother of the sky. A transmission of secret pilot's business I don't really understand, but, somehow, I do.

"You got this," Talon-Two says. "See you on the ground."

The orange glow behind the F35 Lightning-II rockets into a sharp stream of blue turbine-exhaust as his plane pulls up and banks hard left. It disappears from my view in a second.

••••••••••

Passing three thousand, one hundred feet.

I transmit, "Localiser captured. Glideslope indication's coming down."

"Okay," says Anderson. "You know what to do. Flaps thirty. Set speed to one-forty. Check the speed brake is armed, and double-check the auto brake is set to MAX."

I do exactly as he says. "Done. The approach is fully captured, too."

"Good. You're doing great. This is it. Monitor as you descend. At three hundred feet, get your hands ready on the controls, just like we briefed."

He makes it all sound like just another day at work.

....

Perth Airport looks huge now. Approach lights, runway lights, and a bunch of flashing red and blue in the far distance. Emergency vehicles at the far end? Must be.

A new voice booms, "Two thousand, five hundred."

I near jump out of my seat. The creepy voice came from behind and above, and I take a second before I remember it's the automated voice of the GPWS—the ground-proximity-warning-system. And Anderson's words hit my memory: 'When you hear the GPWS call "two thousand, five hundred", that means…'

Suck a big breath through the nasal prongs.

It seems like no time at all before the next callout from the GPWS. "One thousand."

Crunch that urge to cough.

Check the runway ahead.

The autopilot seems to be holding our approach steady, like we're on rails.

"Five hundred."

My hands tremble.

Eyes locked and hard, despite the drops of salty sweat invading them from above. We're still lined up okay, I think.

"Four hundred."

Fire raging in my chest, but *don't cough*, dickhead. Not now.
"Three hundred—"

33

O_2: 2% LOW

The angry readout beside my knee is blinking hard, begging for my attention. I stare at those tiny red numbers. That piss-weak reading of two percent is gonna flip to zero any second now. But my lungs are already there. *They burn.* My body screams for more air—for oxygen.

This isn't the time to be looking down, though. Not now.

I jerk my head upwards. I gotta look … I just have to—

Blink.

Disbelief at the massive sea of lights out there in the dark: white, green, blue, and red. Some are flashing as if sharing the panic with me. A few strobing. Most seem fixed in space and the faraway ones shimmer and shake.

"Now, Dylan. Do it now," Anderson says, his voice even more raspy and strained.

My left thumb is near this tiny black button. Not right on it, but near enough. One press and it will be done. No going back.

More lights are flicking past. Faster. Bright and piercing. A row of pinpoint green ones ahead. There's a dark space behind with lines of tiny white lights out to the horizon, like a freakish oblong-shaped black hole pulling me forward.

"Two hundred," the other voice says again. But, unlike Anderson, this guy still sounds calm. He seems kinda stoned, too, like I remember from years back.

I wheeze in a forced breath until my lungs scream back at me, then chance another quick look down at the bottle:

O_2: 1% LOW

Whatever.

One press of this button near my thumb and it won't matter. Nothing will.

How crazy is this? I spent years dreaming of sitting in this seat, and now I'm finally here. Irony is, this is probably the last thing I'll ever do. I'll most likely be dead within the next minute. My chances of pulling off this crazy manoeuvre? About one-in-four, I reckon.

And even if I do survive, it probably won't matter. I could be dead in twenty-four hours, anyway. My chances of surviving the operation I'm supposed to have tonight are one-in-five.

And if by some miracle I make it through, I'm guessing I'll go six-feet-under within a year. Around half the people like me do.

"Dylan, *now*!" Anderson's lost all his cool. His panic is real, which is nuts, 'coz he's not even here.

The line of green lights is closer now. Really close.

Should I be asking: *why me?* I could ask that question if I had the time. That bitch—that very question—has been following me like a stray dog. Any other dumb prick who found themselves where I am right now, if they were doing what I'm about to do, they'd be asking, *why … the … hell … me …* if they weren't too busy screaming.

Faces float in and out of my head. People who give a damn. People who matter to me. Never thought I'd get all the stuff about others, but maybe … maybe she was right. Just wish I could've told her before—

The green lights flick under the nose.

This is insane. Death is right here, but I feel … alive.

Nothing for it, then.

I press the black button.

34

B*zz, bzz … bzz, bzz.*

What the…?

But it's the 737 telling me the autopilot has released control of the plane—to me.

My right thumb does what it needs to do. There's one more black button to press.

Whoop, whoop, whoop—autothrottle disconnect.

Runway coming up fast. The surrounding airport growing at me like an inflating balloon.

Are we drifting? Slipping left?

I roll the control yoke a bit to the right. Nothing happens.

Roll a bit more. Nothing happens.

WTF? But one of Anderson's coaching lines comes back to me: "At low speed the controls will feel heavy and unresponsive. The plane will fly like a wet blanket, so if you gotta put in a control input, be *assertive* with it. Do it, then count slowly to three."

Slowly? Prick.

Big turn on the yoke to the right. Do what the man said: count to three, and … *response*! I sense a shallow bank to the right.

Runway's more steady, but we're still heading for the left edge.

These controls are nothing like I expected.

"One hundred," the GPWS calls.

This can't be happening.

Another turn right. Struggle to line it up.

Approach lights racing past.

"Fifty."

God.

Big, white, runway markers in the landing lights slip underneath.

My left arm tugs back on the control column. Somehow it remembered to reduce the rate of descent when the 'fifty' callout happened, even if my brain didn't.

But too much?

Not descending now.

Floating.

More runway slipping past below.

Ease the nose down.

Losing height.

Too much?

"Forty."

Slipping further left.

Big turn right.

Wings off-level.

"Thirty."

"F…a…r…k!" I yell to nobody.

"Twenty," the GPWS voice says back, still calm-as.

Slam the thrust levers back to idle.

Still off to the left.

"Ten."

Dropping like a stone.

Bang. The right main wheel hits hard.

A bounce.

Instinct, or a god, or someone, tells me to lower the nose. So I heave the control column forward.

Bang, again, and *screech*. Nosewheel meets bitumen.

Lurch left as the left main wheel slams onto the ground.

Then this insanely loud, electric whir and a sharp bang happens next to my knee as the speed brake handle automatically slams itself into the 'UP' position.

But no time to look down. We're ploughing along the left edge of the runway with grass and crap flashing up past the windows.

I go to slam the right rudder pedal in, but the damn thing feels so stiff and heavy I'm not sure how far I'm even pressing it.

The main gear thumps repeatedly over runway lights, but the sound stops as we swing hard to the right.

Out of control?

Reversers? *Reversers*!

Anderson said nothing about putting the engines in reverse. My right hand fumbles over the top of the thrust levers and down the front as I try to find the reverser levers.

But the laws of physics has other ideas and I'm slammed forward against the seat harness with my head nearly careening into the glareshield.

What the?

My right hand slips off the reverser handles and hits something.

Across now … across the runway centreline. Heading for the right edge.

Hit the left rudder pedal. *Lurch*. Hit it again.

Big swing left.

Gravity rips at me.

Right rudder.

Keep it on the runway.

Slowing? Yes, we're slowing hard. The auto brakes—of course—they're working!

But I'm not taking *no* for an answer. My hand finds those frickin reverser handles again and I reef them both up and back.

The roar of the engines in full reverse behind me is the best thing I ever heard.

But red lights now. A line of red lights ahead.

Other end of the runway? Yes, but still slowing. But I'm on the runway, sort of. Firmly on the ground, though, so don't care.

Heaps of blue and red lights further on. All flashing, like a fuming swarm of bees with party lights.

Look down.

O_2: 0% EMPTY

Goodbye, little mate.

Something pierces in my headset. Anderson's voice, and so high-pitched he sounds like a kid. "The reversers, Dylan. *Stow the reversers*!"

Oops. Do what the pilot man says. Stow those reverser handles back down.

Cockpit noise back to a hum.

We're almost stopped.

Red and blue lights racing towards me.

A zillion thoughts float in chaos.

Things are bright everywhere, but it's fading. Like a tunnel coming to an empty end.

I fumble for the engine start levers with my fingers. Can't really see, so only going by touch. This wasn't an Anderson instruction, but I know what to do.

Sounds are hollow. Empty. Like I'm underwater, at the deep end.

Tunnel smaller. Narrow.

Cough.

Jerk those start levers out and down.

Feel the engine vibrations die.

Wheeze.

Gasp again for air.

Only one sound left now. My own pathetic attempt to inhale.

Cough.

Tunnel ending. Closer.

A face appears in the windshield. A pale vision…

Her.

Wheeze.

And I suddenly understand. Allie is all I—

35

It's like the tide going out.

Part of you becomes exposed above the surface. Light, vibrations, and sensations. You feel the waves of sleep ebb back and away, and then suddenly you're lying exposed on the sand.

You're awake.

Although, there's also a weird millisecond when you think you might be awake but you're not really sure. Like, am I here? Am I still dreaming?

Two round lights blare above me. Runway lights?

Damn it! Hit the brakes!

But my feet only find empty space and the sensation of smooth cool cloth.

All white. I'm lying in soft white. And there're white walls and a matching white ceiling.

No cockpit. No airport.

It makes sense: *I'm dead.*

Yes. It makes perfect sense. Imagine if this heaven stuff was real after all.

Then a *whoosh–hiss* sound, and my nose picks up faint chemical whiffs.

"Welcome back, Dylan."

Huh? Not a voice I recognise. An angel?

"Who is this?" forms in my head, but my throat and mouth won't work.

A hand on my forehead: soft, warm, feminine.

"Don't talk. Take it slow. Real easy now," the voice says.

Easy? Is she kidding me? Turn my head left. Muscles scream. God-awful tube in my mouth makes me want to hurl. Nausea grips.

Whoosh–hiss.

So much for heaven.

But there she is beside me: an angel covered in protective gear, head tilted to one side, concern across her face, her brown eyes searching mine through her plastic face guard.

"You're in the ICU," she says. "I'm Steph, your nurse."

"Uh," is all I can manage.

Definitely not heaven.

Whoosh–hiss.

"Easy now. Take it slow, remember."

I turn my eyes further left, then right, then beyond my feet.

Light-blue curtains everywhere. Carts with gizmos and wires. Yellow bins. Metal stands with plastic bags and tubes hanging. Electronic machines, lots of machines and all beeping for attention. ICU?

She reads my face. "Your operation is all over, Dylan. The transplant. It went fine and you've been out like a light for a long while. It's good to have you back with us."

I go to talk again, but there are still no words. Bloody tube.

"I'll let Professor Hardy know you're awake. She'll be here soon."

Whoosh–hiss.

....

Another hand on my forehead. Different?

Force my eyes to open.

Whoosh–hiss, and something beeping away near my head.

No bad dreams that time. No nonsense about landing a jet. *Jeez.*

"Dylan. I know you can't talk. So nod or whatever, okay?" Professor Hardy says.

I nod.

Pain. *Damn.* Neck and chest muscles tense with heat. Electric pulses. Something sharp in my back. Room swims. Bile grips further down. Resist the urge to heave.

Whoosh–hiss.

"Are you in very much pain?"

I nod, but with much less enthusiasm.

"We'll give you more meds to help with that. The only thing you need to do today is keep still and rest, okay? We'll see if we can get you moving a bit tomorrow."

I stare her hard in the eyes. So much I want to know.

"You sure gave us some interesting moments on your way in," she says.

I have no clear memory, no real idea, what the hell she's talking about.

Whoosh–hiss.

"But the operation went as well as we could hope for. Tomorrow, we'll begin post-op therapy and get you off the ventilator as soon as we can."

The thought hits me. That repeating *whoosh–hiss* sound beside me is the ventilator. I'm not breathing yet—it is.

Whoosh–hiss.

36

Day two

The rest of yesterday? A mixed up blur of crazy. More unknown medications coursing through my veins. Seeing stuff in the room, visions and crap. In and out of sleep. Dumb dreams. Pain constant and in unbelievable waves and peaks every now and then.

They got the intubation tube out this morning and I'm off the friggin ventilator. But, be careful what I wish for…

A therapist—Jacob I think his name is—is working me over. "Take it in slowly, yep. Now, hold it. And out now, nice-n-easy."

Head's swimming. Can I breathe on my own?

Air?

O_2?

Flustered.

Go for a big breath, suck it up. Daggers of pain. Stars in the air like sparklers. And the tunnel's coming back.

"Dylan, Dylan!" his voice calls down the tunnel.

What?

"Another breath, mate, but *easy* with it this time. And use the button under you thumb if you need another hit of the morphine, yeah."

I go to say, "piss off and leave me alone," but only manage a cracked gurgle. My throat screams at me: *don't try that again, dickhead.*

On we go. Every minute is an hour. Every shallow breath a fight for air. Learning how to do it. Learning how *not* to do it.

It all screws with my head. With every breath, I remember these are not my lungs. They're foreign. Someone's dead and I got his parts. But why? How? And what happened to him?

So many questions.

So many tubes.

37

Day three

I finally got to drink something. I actually swallowed some liquid. That's another frickin tube gone, so there's only two more to go now. And they finally got me sitting up. Nearly passed out with the pain, and I spewed a bit of acid, but at least I'm more vertical.

My sense of smell has returned big time, but I wish it had stayed on leave. This place stinks like hell. Other patients are constantly being moved around me and I get these god-awful wafts of body odour, body fluids, disinfectant, something like alcohol, and hospital food. This place is enough to make anyone sick.

I need a distraction. "Can you get me off these drugs," I ask, hardly recognising my voice. "They fully suck."

Professor Hardy smiles a knowing smile. "Ah, no. Your pain meds will be reduced, slowly, but the immunosuppressant and anti-rejection drugs will be part of your routine for life I'm afraid. Better get used to them."

"I hate you."

She chuckles. "How are you sleeping now?"

"Alright. No more weird dreams, thank goodness. Just seeing hazy stuff sometimes."

"Hallucinations and visions are pretty common given the cocktail of drugs you're on. Ride the trip, it'll pass."

"Good. No more nightmares about bloody 737s, then."

She cocks her head to one side and her forehead crumples into wrinkles. "737s?"

"Yeah," I croak, shaking my head. "I dreamt I landed one and saved the day."

She raises her eyebrows, goes over to her bag, and pulls something out. "I'll see you this afternoon." She drops the folded object onto my lap and glides out the room.

A newspaper. But I'm not into news, so I chuck it on the table next to the bed. It flops open and then I see it. Front page, big letters: 'MIRACLE AT PERTH AIRPORT: Passenger lands stricken plane!'

And—

•••••••••••

"Dylan, Dylan, hey mate. Open your eyes."

The tunnel. *Again*? It's like a repeating horror scene.

I recognise her tone. Steph must be back on shift. "What? What ah—"

"You checked out on us again, Dylan. Try not to do that, huh?" she says.

"Um, sorry. I dunno…"

She spies the newspaper headline on the bedside table and points at it. "It's all coming back then?"

"No. Not really. I thought all that business was from your drugs wiping me out."

"Ah, nope. You were too busy being a hero before we got our hands on you, jet-boy. Do you remember much about it?" she asks.

"No."

"Others will fill you in, I'm sure. Later on."

"I need to find out what happened."

"Yeah, I bet. But I'm just your nurse, so—"

"What about the passengers? The crew? Are they okay?"

She clenches her jaw and fiddles with the beeping IV machine above my head. "We'll allow you some visitors, maybe tomorrow. You can ask questions then. But go easy," her voice tapers off, "you gotta focus on you, for now. It's important you stay as positive as you can."

"I need my phone."

"All in good time," she says with a maternal smile.

"How about a TV, then? Come on?"

She says, "Later," and heads into the corridor.

I spot the newspaper in Steph's hand as she walks away. She's doing her best to hide it from my view. Somebody's in control here, but it sure-as-hell isn't me.

••••••••••

Different room now. Same white everything except for a window on one side. Must be late afternoon because the light is soft and blue. And there's a row of glass panels along the internal wall to the corridor.

Steph at the door, "Hey, jet-boy. We got a cast of thousands who want to see you. Are you up for some visitors?"

"I guess."

"Okay, just a second. We can't let them into your room yet, but they can say a quick hello at the window."

It's not long before a line of faces forms in the corridor. Seems like a reverse police lineup, or an aquarium where I'm the fish. Not a cast of thousands, though, but five faces in the line I recognise, and one face I don't.

My hand comes up to signal *hello* as I scan across their faces.

Aunt Cheryl's there. Older now. More wrinkled, but her features are as I remember. God, it's been years.

And Max, the boss of the café in Perth; he's smiling like a cat.

Next to Max, his brother Garry, the manager from our Perth Office.

And there's Greg. Greg from Karratha? *WTF*! He waggles a finger at me and over-does a big wink.

Another guy next to him. Younger. Arms folded loose. He's smirking and gives me a thumbs-up. Green flight suit. Colour insignias and badges. The thought hits me: *Talon-Two*? Must be. Yes, my brother of the sky.

And at the far end, Allie. Her face pale and drawn. Hair a mess. Looks like hell. She lifts her hand and puts it to the glass and half-smiles.

Something breaks, then. Something rips away inside my head. Something grips hard in my guts. It's like I've been running, always running, and that invisible thing has finally got me—it's caught up. My whole being—head, mind, body, the lot—is finally, after all these years, letting go.

I can't run anymore.

I snatch a breath, but it bursts back out as a sob. Like a bomb blast in slow-mo. Tears on a hose. I start to shake. Drop my hand. Drop my head.

What's happening?

Steph takes my dropped hand. She strokes my thumb with her fingers. She waves away those six faces with her other hand, and they're gone, just like that.

"It's okay," she says. "You've been through a heck of a lot. So let it out now. Yeah? It's okay. I'm here."

And as she sits here with me, with my hand shaking in both of hers, the past eight years roll through my mind; even through my uncontrolled sobs. Those faces are no longer at the windows, but it's like they, and others too, are right here in the room.

I think about my mum, and what happened to her, and her flight, and how I got to live at Aunt Cheryl's.

I remember Aunt Cheryl and her escape. About how she had to boot me out of the nest and into the big wide world. Best thing she ever did for me.

The road trip out of Melbourne. The bus. Hitching rides across the country. That George wanker. And, what was the other guy's funny name? Oh yeah, Pothole, picking me up in his truck.

The job with Max in Perth, and his intro to Gavin, and the other work with him.

Nancy? Yeah, Nancy.

Karratha. Taking that crazy chance.

Greg. The one before, and the Greg I know now.

And Alan, my other boss.

Professor Hardy, miracle woman.

And Allie.

And I think, *what if?*

What if I'd headed for Brisbane instead of Adelaide that day? What if I'd turned left, not right, at the bus station in Perth? What if I'd turned down the job in Karratha? What if Allie's sister never had CF? What if my GP had told Allie to piss off? What if Greg hadn't forced me into his car and onto the plane? And what if I'd never known how to fly?

What if?

Did some demented sadomasochist design all this shit, like, especially for me? Has someone been pulling the strings this whole time?

But even if someone, or something, has been deciding my future in the past few days, I've now cheated death not once, not twice, but three times already. So, you know what? Screw him, or her, or it, or them, or whatever. Screw the lot of them.

I'll just *live*, for as long as I can, if that's okay.

38

Day four

Awake.

White room, and in a ward now.

Yep, still here.

Wafts of disinfectant invade my nostrils, plus something sweeter in the mix. I feel my hand wrapped in someone else's.

"Hey."

I recognise this voice. "Hey," I say back.

"You gonna go all salty on us and lose your shit again?" she asks.

I laugh for the first time since I can remember. And for the first time since I can remember, it doesn't make me cough. "Piss off. Who let you in here?"

"Oh, I've got my ways."

"Ain't that the truth."

"You scared the crap out-a-me," she says.

"I scared the crap outa myself."

Allie's eyes widen and her voice softens, "You're … okay, though?"

"I got a long way to go, I think. But yeah, I'm getting there."

She leans forward. "Don't you ever bloody fly a plane again."

"Not if I can help it," I say.

"Good. 'Coz, you got airlines getting '*all competitive*'," she says while making air-quotes with her fingers, "and falling all over themselves to sponsor your flight training."

"What? Jeez. Not a chance."

"Good then."

"So, how'd you hear about all of that?"

"Ah, Dylan," she says, shaking her head, "you don't know it yet, but you're an international superstar, old mate. You're everywhere. If I see your ugly face online or on the tele *once more,* I think I'll puke."

"Um, wow."

She talks on for a while about all the media hype, the headlines, and stories about miracles. A betting agency had given odds of ten-to-one of me making the landing, and some punters had reaped some big winnings that night. A happy-clapper church near Perth Airport claimed it was their prayer meeting at the time which made the difference. And a renowned international clairvoyant had tweeted the universe had told her I'd crash on the runway but I'd survive. Is there such a thing as half-right?

But as Allie rattles it all off, I'm hearing her, but not really listening.

"What about the others … on the plane?"

Allie's head drops. "Um, later. Not now."

"Yes, *now*. Tell me what's happened."

Allie looks around the room and out to the corridor. She bites her bottom lip, then whispers, "It's not real good."

"I want to know. I *have* to know. Please."

"Look, ah … only eight," she gulps and turns back, "only eight people survived. The rest didn't make it. From a lack of oxygen. I'm sorry."

A hundred people on the plane and only eight others had made it. Can this be legit? Is it even possible? As I stare speechless at Allie, the intensity in and behind her eyes tells me I can't ignore these facts, much as I want to.

But why?

Why some people and not others? How? Who's fault? And what for? And why not me?

"The survivors," I whisper back, "Are they okay?"

Allie gulps harder. "Seven are still unconscious and on life support. They might wake up, but the doctors say they could be brain damaged. One guy woke after a few days and they reckon he's gonna be okay."

"Which guy?"

"Dunno, but apparently he was a prisoner, or something."

I remember the guy's snarling face. The cop next to him. The flight attendant. And some of the passengers. I remember my little mate, the oxygen bottle, and the O_2 it gave me, and the CF that made me drag the bottle around to begin with. And I remember how Allie only just missed catching the plane.

She looks out the window and says, "What are the chances?"

My eyes follow hers and all I can do is stare out at the empty blue sky.

39

Day five

Still hurts to talk, but at least I'm eating now. And I woke up bloody starving today. I've never been a big fan of steak, but for some unknown reason all I can think about is half a kilo of prime Wagyu beef cooked medium rare with pepper sauce and a side of mushrooms.

Weird.

They're giving me this clear soup that tastes like second-hand mouthwash, but it's better than syrup down a tube. Not quite Wagyu, but it'll do for now. And the good thing is, that's another one gone. Only a single IV tube left now.

The staff have let a few visitors in today for just a few minutes each. A frickin journalist tried to get into my room this morning, so there's a security guard at the door. And their psych person is working on me twice a day. They seem to think I need the mental support. They could be right.

I met Anderson, the check-and-training captain who'd coached me down. He looks completely different to how I imagined him. I'm glad he's a pilot, 'coz jeez he'd make a crap nurse. He promised to still kick my arse when I'm recovered. And we agreed my landing was, like, the worst ever. I agreed not to fly planes if he promised never to volunteer as a phone counsellor. *Deal.*

And Mr Talon-Two. He brought me in a big autographed print of an RAAF F35, and, thankfully, the weapons bay doors on it were shut tight. His name is Aaron. Yep, a real live human. We're the same age and he grew up near Canberra too. Weird.

Been so good to talk to Aunt Cheryl again, face-to-face. Thought I'd lost all family connection, but it's been there the whole time.

This is all pretty tiring. The fatigue is easing today, but exhaustion is still very much with me. Sleep comes and goes and I've given up fighting it.

I've still got no idea what day it is.

··········

A hand on my shoulder.

Awake, again.

Still here? Yep.

Squint hard now and get these eyes to focus.

A pair of old tan boots on the white hospital floor.

Frayed elastic sides on those boots. There's two legs above—thin denim poles going skyward. A torn knee. A humongous belt buckle.

A chequered shirt is above that buckle. Blue, white and yellow.

Then a skinny black neck.

Then stubble—lots of it. Silver and wiry.

The ceiling lights blast into my eyes from above the stranger's head, so strong I can't really make out his face.

"Thought you hated planes, young fella," he says, as he sits on the chair beside my bed. His half-smile shows some teeth and plenty of gaps in between, and a few more gaps than I remember.

"Hey," I squeak, "yeah, so did I."

"Saw ya picture on the news. I knew it was you. I said to the Mrs, *I know that fella. Found him half-dead on the Nullarbor years ago.*"

I give a strangled laugh.

"Who woulda thought, a white kid running from something, and with no real plans, ends up doin' what you did. How's that happen?"

"It's another one of my l-o-n-g stories."

"I'll bet." His smile is broad. "But that's for another day. You just forget all that and work on getting better, ay? There ain't no need to run anymore."

I nod.

"We'll talk more another time, about your plans."

"Plans?"

He leans his head to one side and his left eye tightens-up as he rubs his chin. "Six days ago you was the right man, right place, right time. You reacted to the stuff happening to ya and you did good. Real good."

"Yeah. It all just … happened."

He shakes his head, "Some of it happened 'coz you made it happen. There was only one person doin' something in that cockpit."

I shrug.

He stretches his neck sideways and uses his head to point towards Allie, who's leaning against a wall out in the corridor. She's eyes down and lost in her phone. "Some things … some things you don't wait to see what happens. None of us know how long or short life's gonna be." He points with his head again, but more pronounced this time. "Some things you get on with and you make 'em happen. You put your past away and you say, ya know what, stuff the risk. Time and chance and all that shit can go get rooted."

"Oh. Right. So, who you been talking to?" I say, doing my best not to smile.

"Never you mind," he chuckles, "but I better get going. Nurse's orders, you know."

"It's good to see you again."

"And you, my boy." He turns at the door. "Good thing is, you've had way more than your fair share, Dylan. Things will only get better from here."

I remember those words and can't help cracking a smile. "Who says?" I ask, parrot-like.

He winks at me before he disappears into the corridor.

"Pothole says."

NIC D'ALESSANDRO
WRITER

Thank you for reading O_2

If you enjoyed this book, please spread the word by posting a review (brief and informal is fine) at amazon.com, goodreads.com, or any website where good books live.

Your feedback, comments, and questions are welcome by email and on my social media pages – see nicdalessandro.com/contact. If you post a review on social media, please use the tag #O2thenovel

Bonus content for readers

You're invited to access reader-only content for this book, including background to the story, how it was produced, the characters, and behind-the-scenes elements – nicdalessandro.com/O2-bonus-content

More for you to read and enjoy

Please visit nicdalessandro.com to check out my other books.

Subscribe to my newsletters at nicdalessandro.com/subscribe to be in the know about my upcoming books and offers—including further books in the *Dylan Malloy* series.

Proceeds from O_2 to fund medical research

A donation from the sale of each paperback and ebook will be donated to *Cystic Fibrosis Australia* (a registered charity) to fund support for people with cystic fibrosis and medical research.

You can help in the fight against CF

Cystic fibrosis (CF) is a very real yet not widely known disease. There are at least 105,000 people currently diagnosed with CF across the world, including over 3,600 people in Australia alone. CF management and treatment is improving, but still has a long way to go. The challenges CFers have to deal with every day—as Dylan showed us in the story—are many and varied. And the average life expectancy for CFers is still way too short.

Research into CF and programs to support CFers are making a real difference in people's lives, including the families and friends who support them. You and I can partner in this vital work by donating funds to the peak CF organisation in your region.

Please donate what you can to:

Australia: cysticfibrosis.org.au
Canada: cysticfibrosis.ca
Europe: cf-europe.eu
New Zealand: cfnz.org.nz
United States: cff.org
United Kingdom: cysticfibrosis.org.uk

or search 'cystic fibrosis' in your region.

About VATSIM – the International Online Aviation Network

The VATSIM organisation Dylan refers to in this book is real. VATSIM is a non-profit organisation dedicated to the provision of a free online flight-simulation network.

Every day, thousands of volunteers from all over the world interact in the simulated aviation world VATSIM creates on the Internet. The platform entertains, informs, and educates many people of all ages and backgrounds, and incredibly, all at no-charge to the users. Some of VATSIM's users go on to become real-life pilots or air traffic controllers in the aviation industry—just how Dylan himself had intended.

To find out more, please visit vatsim.net

Donations to support VATSIM Inc. can be made at: donorbox.org/donate-to-vatsim

Acknowledgements

I simply couldn't write my books alone without the support and expertise of other people, and this book has been another top-notch team effort.

Thank you to my trusty beta readers: Ben Ippolito, Julie Poole, Jen Hauser, Donita Shadwick, Rosalie Bouwmeester, and Kent Whitmore; and to my ever-wonderful alpha reader, Frances D'Alessandro. Your tireless reading of my drafts, your feedback, and your encouragement have been instrumental in the development of this book.

I had incredible input and support from subject matter experts in the field of cystic fibrosis (CF). A huge thanks to Jen Hauser for your clinical and personal expertise on CF, and to Paula Wriedt of *Cystic Fibrosis Tasmania* for your help finding information and contributors for the book. Thanks to Carrie Leppard for your support and the connections you made for me with people in the CF community.

A big thank you to Jack, Meg, Sarah, and Steve who all gladly gave up their time to share their personal experiences of CF. Your openness and generosity was amazing, and I learned so much about what it's like to live with CF from our long chats. And by the way, there's a little of each of you in Dylan's character, and at least one quote from each of you in his dialogue—see if you can find it!

On the aviation side-of-things, I was ably assisted by air-traffic-controller (ATC), pilot, and good friend—Ben Ippolito. Thanks, mate, for your real-life ATC and airline operations expertise, and for the great insights about living in Karratha, WA.

Thanks so much to Peter O'Connor from *Bespoke Book Covers* for the awesome cover design, and for donating your time and expertise for the CF cause.

Thank you to Donita Shadwick (and Kent) for proofreading the manuscript. So glad you came back for another round! Really appreciate your time and expertise.

Last, and certainly not least, I'd like to thank my amazing editor, Kelly Rigby. You took the story and the characters under your wing and helped bring them to full life. I think there were some points where you understood Dylan better than me! I have learned so much from working with you, Kelly, and I'm so glad we connected on this project.

To all of you, including anyone I've missed, and to all the friends and family members who took an interest and encouraged me along the way, I thank you.

March 2023

Nic D'Alessandro

About the author

Born and bred on an island state, Nic D'Alessandro is passionate about the wilderness, sea, and sky. He's a writer, photographer, and education consultant who is fascinated by the human condition, and anything that floats or flies.

Nic is a keen sailor, and when he's not on the water, he takes to the sky in aircraft whenever he can. He obtained his pilot licence at age seventeen, and later celebrated his forties by building a full-size 737 flight simulator in his garage.

Prior to writing fiction, Nic forged a career as an education leader, manager in the public sector, and specialist in the aviation industry. He's now channelling his life and career experiences into written works to entertain, surprise, and stimulate thought.

Nic lives in Tasmania, Australia with his wife, and extended family.

NIC D'ALESSANDRO
WRITER

Made in the USA
Monee, IL
14 August 2023

41010692R00152